# Gangsta City

**Lock Down Publications
Presents
Gangsta City
No Loyalty. No Luv.
A Novel by *Duke***

# Lock Down Publications
P.O. Box 1482
Pine Lake, Ga 30072-1482

**Lock Down Publications**
**Like our page on Facebook: Lock Down Publications @**
www.facebook.com/lockdownpublications.ldp
Cover design and layout by: **Dynasty's Cover Me**
Book interior design by: **Shawn Walker**
Edited by: **Mia Rucker**

Duke

# Prologue

"*Rocks. Blows.*" Shouts echoed throughout a tight cluster of sixteen-story high rises.

"*Weed. Pill. If you gotta junky, we gotta banana fo' that monkey.*"

The volumes on the voices were cranked up to be heard, but the faces behind them were kept hidden and unseen, all tucked inside the shadows of doorways and dark corners. The fast-talking spiels were aimed at the tweaking cluckas and sick fiends who swarmed the projects like zombies. Most came on foot from different directions, but a few pulled up in rusty traps, some hustling, some tricking, all of them spending.

The man behind one of the voices stood half-hidden in a doorway. He was working point for a young crew who wrote his sales pitch to milk the building for everything it was worth, and they were holding it down with everything they had. The man spotted a customer, one of their regulars, headed his way, and he seemed drawn to the shouts like a hungry mutt to a dinner bell.

Omar was the customer's name, and his monkey was a gorilla. Six-four and every bit of two-fifty, once upon a time the thirty-something-year-old had a fierce reputation for breaking jaws and cracking teeth. That was back in his heyday, when he was known as Bone Crusha. But those days of his gangsta were long gone - part of the history books - and the new breed of youngsters saw him as just another one of the walking dead infesting the streets like a virus.

Hands buried deep in his pockets, Crusha's twitchy eyes scanned left and right for any sign of onetime lurking in a cut and ready to jump out for a quick bust. Trying his best to blend in with traffic, he ignored the advertising campaigns from the other high-rises nearby as he made a b-line through a crowded parking lot towards his favorite doorway. When he got close, the man hiding in the shadows stepped halfway out and greeted him with a menu.

"Asswipe blows and Green Monsta rocks." Their special of the day was heroin and cocaine.

The street lights buzzing high over the lot barely exposed an all-black outfit, a face covered by a ski mask, and a White Sox cap cocked sideways. The man didn't bother with instructions since all their customers already knew the drill.

Crusha raised his hands and the masked man proceeded with the customary pat down, searching for guns, knives, or anything that looked police issued. Then he gave the usual warning.

"Keep hands outta pockets, money in hands, and money unfolded at all times."

Crusha stepped inside then hesitated just long enough for his eyes to adjust in the inky darkness of a long hallway. A few feet away, a tall figure emerged like a black ghost fitted in the same project issued uniform as the man at the door, matching mask included.

"Blows and rocks on three, weed and pills up top," the dark figure spoke.

The building's floors were like aisles in a Wal-Mart, and the man in black was customer service. Besides directing traffic, he handled all issues and complaints with a baseball bat leaning against a wall just out of sight - no returns.

The only issue Crusha had was getting his fix, and he didn't need directions either. The dope fiend shopped there all the time and he knew his way around just fine. But, when he stepped into the stairwell going up, he ran into a traffic jam he wasn't expecting. Other customers, addicts of every kind, were packed bumper to bumper, standing sweaty, smelly, and anxious in a long line spiraling up while they waited to make their purchases.

"Dam," Crusha was hoping to get in and out. He lost track of how many hours had passed since he last fed his habit, and withdrawal symptoms were ringing in his head like an alarm clock. The knuckles of an eight hundred pound gorilla were tapping impatiently on his shoulder and whispering in his ear, "Ay, Omar, you ain't fo'get about me, did ya?"

The fiend wiped the sweat off his bald head and nervously glanced down at a pair of wrinkled twenties in his hand. He rubbed them between his fingers, double and triple checking the cheap ink and paper they were printed with.

"Damn," Crusha was still cussing, and he was having really bad feelings about that one. He might've lost the sharp edge to his instincts years ago - right after he sucked his first hit through a car antenna - but his better judgment was tickling the hairs on the back of his neck with a warning nonetheless.

About fifteen minutes ago, he was stalking gas stations over on the Ave, sizing up purses to snatch or cars to jack, when he ran into one of his old partners from the other side of the projects. "Dirty Red" was what they called him. High-yellow with freckles, Red's look matched his name to a T, and he wore the "Dirty" like a badge of honor. He was a character straight out of a comic book, the villain everybody loved to hate, and Crusha usually avoided making deals with snakes like him. But the slimy nigga's offer was too good to pass up.

"Man, Crusha, I gotta rack of bogus dubs hot off the presses. You put in that work and we can both get straight."

They both knew Red's rep around the projects was always suspect, and their chances at passing the bills would be better with Crusha behind the transaction.

"Fitty-Fitty?" Crusha was no sucka.

"No doubt." Red set the hook by adding, "Easy money, like candy from a baby. Betta than boost'n or rob'n ol' ladies."

The truth of those words stung Crusha worse than a thousand cigarette burns. The dope fiend's hustles to come up had been falling short all that day. His first early-morning plot got foiled after he had to drag somebody's granny damn near half a block before she finally let go of her purse straps. Then his bad luck turned buzzard when a couple bystanders turned his smooth getaway into a frantic scramble. They chased him over a fence and he fumbled the goods. A simple strong-armed robbery turned into a blank mission.

Crusha kicked himself in the ass for hours after that, until he decided to roll the dice at a liquor store downtown. His luck was no better, though, and he wound up making another mad dash when a nosey clerk peeped him stuffing his straight legs with Grey Goose and tried to pinch him at the door. The bottles all busted in the tussle and he had to make that getaway empty handed.

Over an hour later, there he stood in the stairwell still smelling like Vodka, and the closer he inched his way to the top, the more frantic he got for the fix. But with most of the day gone, he knew if his latest scam didn't work, the gorilla beating on his back would make him tap out, too weak to hit the streets and hustle.

"*Asswipe. Green Monsta. Rick James.*" A small group of servers at the third floor landing were advertising their brand names for the customers, and they had orders moving in and out more efficiently than a drive-thru at McDonalds.

The customer up front ordered. "Gimme four Green Montas."

Behind him, "Two Asswipes."

Next, "One and one."

A cute young chick who looked way too young and cute to be a dope fiend pulled in and placed her order.

"One Ricky and wipe his ass two times." She stuffed the bags in her bra and left. Crusha's turn was up.

"Who you want playa?" The man closest to the steps was spitting out dimes from behind his ski mask while his buddies around him counted money. Another man lurked in the background, leaning incognito against a wall with a hand wrapped around something with a trigger on it.

All of them were separated from the crowd on the steps by a stolen shopping cart filled with bricks, cinder blocks, and broken chunks of concrete. The cart was their check-out counter, and the bullshit inside was an emergency brake ready to tumble down on the local stick-up men bold enough to commit a robbery, or any police dumb enough to rush up the stairs on a bust.

"Three Asswipes and a Montsa." Crusha quickly handed over the two dubs then made like he was in a hurry, bouncing from foot to foot and silently praying that the man didn't pay too much attention to the paper. But instead of praying for luck, and before he took Red up on his offer, he should've done some homework on how many times that slimy nigga burned this spot with his funny money.

The cashier behind the register flicked on a small flashlight. Crusha's heart sank to his stomach and skipped a few beats.

"Nigga, what the fuck is this?" That wasn't really a question, and the man wasn't really looking for an answer, but his words did get the attention of buddy behind him with the banger.

"Gangsta, hold this nigga while I check his funds." The man in the background didn't hesitate to step up and press the cold barrel of a four-nickel to the middle of Crusha's sweaty forehead.

"Move and I'm knock'n yo shit back." The silence and darkness in the stairwell made the youngster's bark sound worse than a bite.

Panic began to rise through the customers on the steps behind Crusha. Some of the slow thinkers at the front of the line started asking, "Man, can I get mine befo you kill this fool?"

The ones towards the back were quicker on their feet. They mumbled in the middle of their U-turns, "Man, I'm gett'n the fuck outta here."

"Everybody shut the fuck up," the man with the bullets ordered with a click-clack of his hammer.

A quick glance at the bills told his partner the serial numbers matched the same twenties they had been getting burned with all week, and they had been waiting for a nigga to try them again. He blew a two fingered whistle down the stairwell to a few of their guys posted in spots only they knew about.

Crusha spit out an *Oh shit* as terror flooded his gut and turned shit into bubbles. Even though the gangster formally known as Bone Crusha no longer existed, and those youngsters were a different kind of breed from a whole new generation, the justice system in the projects was still old-school and plea bargains were never part of a deal.

Instead of trying to beg his way out of a situation too sticky for words, the dope fiend pulled together whatever strength he had left, sent a quick shout out to God just in case he still had an ear open for a nigga's prayers, and then let his instincts do the talking for him.

Crusha's left arm swung up like a heavy club and knocked the gun away from his face. An eye blink later, his right fist followed and slammed a solid upper cut to the man's chin. The big four-nickel bucked like thunder and lit up the stairwell with a blinding flash. Nap time for the young gangster behind the trigger, he fell asleep on his feet and dropped like a rock.

Crusha knew he better get it while the getting was good. He pushed past the spooked customers and took flight down the steps five and six at a time, landing after landing, all the way down to the first floor. Security was posted at the back entrance where he came in, so that was a no go. He rerouted his getaway towards the front, bent a left in the hallway, and cut through the lobby where he could finally see the glow of street lights outside. That's when he ran face-first into the fat end of an aluminum baseball bat.

The sound of a loud "*plink*" echoed through the lobby. That was the aluminum vibrating off his face. A split second later, the "plink" was followed by a meaty "*smack.*" That was the back of his head slamming into the concrete floor. The rest of the action downshifted for Crusha, from real-time to slow motion, as a gang of Nike swooshes rained down on him from all sides and every direction.

Crusha always knew his struggles with addiction must come to an end one day. He just wanted to milk the fun while the party lasted, but he never figured that his ending would be so painful.

Suddenly, something gave the fiend a sliver of hope to grasp at. The bat held its next swing and the Nike swooshes paused in mid-flight. A pair of rubber soles, Jordan's, stood down and spoke up. "Hold up, G. Here comes my mans an'em."

Crusha rolled over broken and bleeding, and with the sting of tears blurring his vision, he struggled to focus on a pair of dark figures stepping through the front entrance. The first man inside turned out to be another one of his old homies, a twenty year nigga who he pulled a few crazy stunts with back in the day. "Knuckles" was what he went by, and the name needed no explanation.

Crusha hatched a quick plan to beg for his life while he still had it. He had just got caught trying to rob a gangster's cookie jar, and project justice had a 99.9% conviction rate, no probation.

"Knuck, my dude," before he could finish, his words were cut short when he got a better look at the second figure stepping into the lobby. He was one of a pair of twins who had a couple of hellified reputations around those projects.

"Man, Fool, no harm no foul," Crusha tried to switch tactics but he got the brothers mixed up and called the wrong name. If a dope fiend didn't have bad luck, he wouldn't have any luck at all. Either way, his plea got choked off by his own blood and a piece of tooth that slipped down his throat.

"Gangsta, what's the word on this nigga?" The youngster with the bat was itching to knock another one out of the park.

Silence seemed to pause time in the lobby, making seconds feel like minutes. Crusha could only hear the tick-tock of his heart beating in his chest and the rustle of curtains slowly closing on the story of his life. Finally, the twin spoke.

"No probation."

Duke

# Chapter One

The alarm on D'mico's body clock rang inside his head and popped open his eyes as if they were riding hydraulics. He sat up in bed, blinked back the fog of sleep, and waited a few seconds for his blurry vision to clear. He set his body to "penitentiary time" six years ago, and his alarm had been going off at the same time every morning since.

"Sleep late, lose weight" was the way of life inside the joint, and even though he got sprung from that cage a few days ago, he was still struggling to shake that mentality and get used to a new reality back in the free world. Now he was waking up in a real bedroom on a real mattress, no plastic, and the naked chick lying next to him was real, too. She was a welcome home present from her to him, and he'd been unwrapping her for three days straight.

D'mico cracked a greedy smile at the sexy curves tangled in sheets that got twisted some time during the night. The warm light shining through the bedroom's only window had her dark complexion looking more intoxicating than a bottle of black Jamaican rum, eighty proof, and he was loving the hangover.

He slid off the bed without disturbing the sleeping beauty, grabbed his phone from the charger on the floor, and then quietly made his way to a chair sitting by the window. After knocking a Newport from a pack and sparking a lighter, he pulled back the curtain to get a good view of Chicago as a new day came to life outside.

Straight ahead, the sun was just beginning to peek its shining head over the silver glass and black steel of the downtown skyscrapers off in the distance. Closer to home, left and right, the rays of morning light were slowly pushing through a gritty haze hovering above a crowded skyline of high-rise project buildings standing tall like giants made of brick and casting long shadows across expanses of cratered asphalt, cracked sidewalks, and grassless dirt littered with garbage of every kind.

Cabrini Green was the concrete jungle where D'mico Barksdale was born thirty-three years ago. "Gangsta City" was what he called the land he'd been claiming ever since, and "Fool" was what the land called him. He took a minute to listen in on the sounds of rush-hour traffic buzzing by down below where the streets were packed with 9 to 5'ers on their way to punch clocks and the sidewalks were thick with hustlers coming off all-night grinds. In the buildings all around him, neighborhood D-boys were scrambling to set up their shops to catch every dollar being spent and the local addicts were clucking like pigeons for any crumbs.

Fool switched his attention back to the bed and the gorgeous body he spent the last few days getting to know so well. When he closed his eyes, he could still taste the sweetness of her pink candy lingering on the tip of his tongue. He could even still feel the softness of her chocolate melting in his hands.

Tameeka Thomas was her name, and he lucked up on the twenty-six-year-old cutie about a year ago when fate made their paths cross through a picture. Her brother happened to be doing a stretch in the same joint and he sent her a flick of them mobbed up and flexing on the weight yard. She dug the cameo and wanted an introduction.

They started getting to know each other through kites, more pics, and occasional collect calls. Fool liked her look right away, from her face to her waist, and she had the kind of thickness a picture couldn't do justice for. He even complimented her for keeping it conservative on the hair weave and leaving some of the tail on the horse. Personality told the rest of her story. She knew how to use what God blessed her with, and she could hold her own, no scavenging.

At the same time, Tameeka was on the other end of the flicks feeling him the same way. The weight yard was doing Fool's body good. His muscles were stacked tight and the sun was kissing the cuts on a complexion barely lighter than hers. He kept his waves low, lined around strong features and a pair of eyes so deep they killed her plans to play hard-to-get.

Over the phone, Fools confidence and educated slang got her impressed with his conversation. And before long, she wanted to know if his physical swag could get her hooked. That's when the postman got ditched, their calls got rerouted, and conversations turned into face-to-face visits.

At that stage in the game, most lifers would've kept their pen-pal spinning like tops with scripts like, "I only got a couple years left," designed to keep the visits coming and the money orders checking in on their books, at least until the woman finally realized the nigga was never coming home and she was nothing more than a long-distance victim. At the time, Fool's circumstances were looking a little rosier than that and he decided to keep it one hundred, so he filled her in on the whole story.

Six years earlier, he and his twin were pumping fiends out of a building in Gangsta City, 1230 Larrabee, the Himalaya. At the time, they were living the fab-life, the fast way, but they started slipping and not paying enough attention to the details. One day a big dent got knocked out of their pockets by a bunch of funny money going around, and when their workers caught a thirsty customer trying to pass a couple dubs, his brother over-reacted and shot the nigga ten times with a forty.

Luck had its back turned on Fool that day, and right before the first shot was fired, a nosy resident overheard the victim say his name. Unfortunately, the man happened to be begging for his life when he said it. Fool was snatched up by the cops, fingered in a line up, and found guilty twelve months later by nine whites, two Asians, and one Uncle Tom. The judge was laughing when he threw the whole book at the twin, life with no parole. That was the beginning of the end for D'mico Barksdale, or so they thought.

Tameeka thought that was terrible, and of course she had questions for him.

"Appeal?"

"So far so good." The appellate court had already ruled in Fool's favor and his case was coming up for a new trail soon.

"Any little Fool's running around?"

"Nope."

"Brother's name?"

"D'mone, but they call him Run Thang." Fool ran down the short version of their family history,

Momma was an addict who never met a drug she didn't like, and banging needles was her favorite way to indulge. She wound up popping a hot dose of heroin back when the twins were still conversing in baby talk. She didn't make it to see them take their first baby steps.

Pops was M.I.A. from the gate, so granny stepped up to the plate and pinch-hitted the best she could. But her ticker was already working overtime and she ended up punching her last clock before she could see them into the first grade.

Tameeka was captivated by Fool's story and she dug a little deeper.

"Foster homes?"

"Cabrini Green was the foster home, Gangsta Disciple was the family."

"Why they call y'all Fool and Run Thang?"

"We got the names we were given."

Back then everyone knew one brother was a thinker with a personality that made people fall in line and follow. The other brother didn't give a fuck about nobody but himself, and he was a damn fool. Problem was, no one could ever tell who was who, so the twins let them get it twisted on purpose and kept up the act in case they ever needed a case of mistaken identity. That scam eventually got ex-ed when Run Thang caught his first set of scars, stitches, and bullet wounds. Tatts did the rest to tell them apart, but by then their names were already stuck.

Tameeka had heard about the special bonds between twins, and she was curious.

"Same thoughts, same feelings?"

"Not exactly," Fool was always calm, cool, and collected, and he never worked off of feelings. Before he pulled a trigger, or threw rocks at the penitentiary, he did his homework and calculated every move from every angle.

Run Thang was just the opposite. His mentality came straight from the planet of the apes. He thought he was the only real gorilla in the flick and everyone else was just wearing costumes. Plus, he reacted off of jealousy and was spontaneous in the worst way. No one ever knew how he'd maneuver when situations got tight.

D'mico and D'mone understood each other because they were brothers from the same struggle. By the time they grew into their roles as Fool and Run Thang, they stayed partners out of necessity, and they recognized it for what it was – no love, no loyalty.

By this chapter in the twin's story, Tameeka already knew which character she liked and which one she didn't.

"If you didn't trust him, what happened to all your stuff?"

"The usual, whips, clothes, and the occasional ho, in that order. Run Thang got the scraps."

"Twin still lookin' out?"

"Hell naw." Back then, Fool's brother had a bad habit of getting him mixed up in his messes. Right before he got popped for that murder, Run Thang had fucked around and planted a seed inside a west-side tramp he couldn't control. He dealt with the situation the only way he could think of at the time. He sent word through some mutual homies that he got killed in a car accident- D.U.I., closed casket.

Shorty was devastated and immediately reached out to Fool, but he didn't feel like covering for his twin on that one and he exposed the bullshit for what it was. Run Thang didn't find out who dropped that dime until Fool was already down for the count. Feeling stabbed in the back, he cut off all ties with his only brother and faded into the background, out of site out of mind.

Tameeka understood perfectly. It was crazy what family would fall out about. To the outsiders looking in, most squabbles seemed like petty shit. But to the brothers and sisters doing the feuding, shit was serious as a heart attack. Either way, she appreciated the honesty and decided to keep it real with him as well.

Tameeka was from a south-side project, Stateway Gardens. She lived with her moms and a beautiful two-year-old daughter named Tamia, who everyone called "Mini Me" because she kept her stuck to her side like glue and always dressed alike. Tameeka's baby's daddy had just gone down on a fresh nickel, and yes, she considered herself a loyal chick and had her man's back, good or bad, wrong or right. But she was an independent mommy before he went AWOL, and she'd still be independent when he got out.

That's when Tameeka made Fool an offer only a fool would refuse. If he came home on appeal, they could be buddies, no strings, whatever happened, happened.

"Fuck buddies?" Fool was definitely not a fool.

"Yup," Tameeka didn't get it twisted. Only dumb bitches with no life stayed faithful to niggas locked up in the slammer. She had better things to do with her life, and her world wasn't getting put on hold for nobody, sorry.

Of course Fool said, "Hell yeah." And as things turned out,, destiny was smiling down on them both. Four days ago, he was knocking out super-sets in the gym when he was called to the warden's office. Word had just come in from the appellate court and it was all good. The only eye-witness testimony got tossed out because she couldn't tell the twins apart in a lineup. And since there were no other witnesses, statements, or physical evidence tying him to the murder, the state of Illinois didn't want to waste time and money putting on a new trial.

Less than twenty-four hours later, Fool was kicked out the front gate of a maximum security prison with twenty-five dollars and a bus ticket. It was as if he was thrown from a world rotating in slow-motion into one spinning at full speed, and he was just starting to feel like he was ready to catch up with traffic.

Fool's thoughts got pulled back into the present when his phone vibrated in his lap. Tameeka was on point with the pre-paid when he touched down, unlimited talk, text, and web. He set the ringtone to "cha-ching" like a cash register, but it was turned off so it wouldn't wake them up. The caller ID popped up "Knuck" with a pair of red boxing gloves.

"What up, Gangsta?" Fool kept his voice low.

Knuck was short for knuckles, and he was a Barksdale from a close branch of the family tree. He got his name from a reputation earned early in his career as a knock out specialist, one and done, and the scarred knobs on his ashy, black fists were the stamps that certified his tittle.

Cuz always kept a one-bedroom on reservation in 624 Division, the Carter, and he donated the tenth floor apartment to Fool as part of a blessing that came with some work for his hand and paper for his pocket.

"You still wrapped in that pussy?" Knuck was always straight to the point.

"Tighter than a hostage." There was never any shame in Fool's game.

Six calendars down state had the twin's moves rustier than Rampage Jackson trying to make a comeback. Lucky for him, Tameeka didn't mind being his sparring partner, and she helped him tighten up his ground-game. Last night he had her twisted in more knots than a pretzel.

"I'm on the breezeway. Come blow one wit me." =Knuck had been trying to talk Fool out of his hiding spot beneath Tameeka ever since he touched down in his plain-Jane Reeboks and gray prison sweats.

"On the way." Fool disconnected, snuffed out his Newport, and then stepped into a pair of shorts and some kicks. At the front door, he slid off the security chain, knocked back the deadbolt, and then headed down the hallway to a fenced-in breezeway overlooking the heart of Gangsta City, high enough to see and stay unseen.

Knuck already had a couple lawn chairs set up like Lay-Z-Boys, a cup of Remy Red on ice, and a grape Swisha on fire. Fool copped a seat and pressed recline.

"Luv for the gifts." The twin definitely needed assistance getting the tools, but he damn sure wouldn't need any help using them to lay his own foundation.

"No doubt," Knuck choked back a cloud of smoke as he passed the B and the cup. "You ready to get back in the lab, mad scientist?"

Fool coughed out a laugh then washed it down with a swig of Remy. Long stretches in a slammer could make an amateur tapout, but he was a decorated vet from the original war on drugs, and he earned his stripes way back when crack first hit Chicago like a terrorist attack and heroin was causing more casualties than suicide bombers.

"Yeah, I used to think I was the Frankenstein of the game." Fool had a PHD in chemistry, and he earned his degree one experiment at a time—bay jars to Pyrexes, microwaves to George Forman's. Once upon a time, he was running through baking soda like Arm & Hammer, plastic baggies like Glad.

While Fool was in the kitchen perfecting the recipes, he was smart enough to realize that everyone in the projects was doing the same basic shit—cop, chop, and serve—nothing special or slick about it. Even the connects were all the same. What separated the Barksdales from the other cliques was they were light on their feet, quick to react to changes in the game, and willing to step on toes when necessary, necks if that's what it took.

Competition bred imagination and dictated tactics, from dimes all day and nicks after midnight to buy one get one Saturdays and bitches get high for half-off Sundays. Fool had more catchy slogans than an infomercial, and he used every trick in the book to pump up their clientele. But "the game is to be sold" was a true story in Cabrini, and he never passed out tips for free.

While he masterminded the business model, Knuck and Run Thang ran the rest of the team, and they had the franchise clicking like clockwork. In the beginning, they used the neighborhood's young wanna-be's to take turns working spots with mouthfuls of bags and spitting at cluckers who walked up. When the police started flipping their flunkies into informants, Knuck was quick to peep that weakness and plug those leaks. He consolidated their hustle inside of the buildings and hired the local addicts to serve up the hand to hand transactions. They were easily replaceable. When one got popped, they switched them out like used batteries and kept the dope lines moving.

Meanwhile, Run Thang took security more seriously than the secret service. He posted lookouts in four-hour shifts around the clock, on every corner, inside buildings and on rooftops with binoculars and two-way radios from Radio Shack. They kept one eye out for the police, the other eye on the workers, and at the same time protected the customers from each other. For the first time, the crack heads and fiends finally felt safe enough to come in and shop without getting robbed on the way out.

Now, according to Knuck, free enterprise was still more popular than video games, and getting it by any means necessary was the only way to play. But recent competition was thick and profits were tight. Instead of sweating that daily grind, Knuck was renting out floors in the Carter for a fee, and he let the new jacks fight over the scraps. It was a lot easier to get the youngsters checking in while he cashed out. But the game was also drawing in new players who were never invited to the table. Cuz gave Fool a heads up on the crooked cops circling the projects like vultures, and how they swept down for a cut as soon as a spot got hot and started making too many moves.

"Yo pockets get'n picked?" Fool looked cuz in the eye, trying to spot the whole truth and nothing but the truth.

"Hell naw," Knuck choked and spit, then he passed the ass-end of the soggy Swisher. "But twin is play'n cops and robbers outta 630 tho."

Fool cocked one eyebrow in surprise. He had heard about his brother relocating his shop over to 630 Evergreen, the 30 Block, but he never would've thought Run would team-up with dirty detectives. That didn't mean he was impressed, though. But the news definitely gave him some serious shit to think about.

"Who's the scoundrel, who's the sucka?" The twin only had a couple questions for the moment.

"Still tryna put a finger on that one. Long as they don't get in my way, everything is peaceful." Cuz had that "fuck them" look on his face.

"Daily bread?" Fool ignored it, but he still knew better.

"They got their shit classified top secret. But the way traffic is movin', they gotta be pumpin' it harder than Denzel pumped that Blue Magic." Knuck offered Fool a refill for his cup, but the twin declined.

No doubt Fool's palms were itching to stamp his own name brand on some of those profits, but his six year hiatus dulled his instincts and he knew better than to throw his chips all in without getting a feel for the hand he was holding.

"Fuck what they doin' anyway. We about to make our own moves, and real gangstas move in silence."

"Ghost?" That was the kind of talk that could hold Knuck's interest.

"Now you see me, now you don't. But that's business for business hours." Fool stood up, stomped out the Swisher, and shook off some ashes. "Right now is play-time, and I gotta new toy I ain't done break'n in yet."

"You gonna get back at twin for leaving a nigga hang'n?" If a war was coming, Knuck had already picked his side.

Fool hesitated, but only for a second. Hate could make most niggas OCD with thoughts of revenge, but his personality wasn't that easily influenced.

"Naw, I'm good on that nigga."

Fool gave cuz the deuces and promised to hit his caller ID later. He made a b-line for the apartment. After double locking the front door and plugging his phone back into the charger, he kicked off his jumpers, stepped out of his shorts, and then woke Tameeka with a smack on her sexy ass.

"Time for another round." He tossed her a pack of condoms from the dresser - glow in the dark blue with ribs. Then he helped her slide one on.

Duke

# Chapter Two

The long days of summer were starting to heat up and the blocks were getting hot in Cabrini. Early morning, before the city cut the switch on the street lights, the neighborhood was already crowded with petty hustlers grinding it out for every penny passing through. Sidewalks and fire lanes were clogged with boosters peddling everything from hats and socks to bottled water and M&M's, all knocked fresh off of store shelves and priced to go.

The parking lots were just as packed with addicts of all kinds, some pretending to be mechanics doing brake jobs and crawling under cars to support their habits, others with less talent prowling for victims and preying on the weak. The corners were staked out by the local riff-raff mingling with a handful of visiting hoodlums. A few vets schooled the new jacks to new games, and the rest were just looking for some bullshit to get into.

Fenced-in between the 30 Block and 1340 Larrabee, a building known as the "Fab 40," sat one of Gangsta City's playgrounds. But the only things to play with were a rusty sliding board that leaned broken to one side, a swing set with no swings, and a sandbox filled with so much dog shit and glass all the kids knew better than to stick their hands in that mess. Nevertheless, a small group of children were happily at play with their mothers standing close by on the lookout for predators. Everyone's reflexes were tuned in for the sound of gunshots, ready to snatch up toys and haul ass.

In the lot behind the 30 Block, Run Thang leaned lazily against the grill of a baby-blue box Chevy, bass humming from the trunk as he flipped through pics on his phone.

A few days ago, he and his crew were bird-watching on the lakefront when he spotted a neat suburban chick sunbathing in a two-piece. Last night she uploaded some back shots to his Facebook. The twin kept his photo albums organized by body-type, and he filed her under "thoroughbred" because she was a runner with an ass like a racehorse.

A few feet to Run's left, one of his main go-to guys stood low-key in the shade on his P's and Q's for any bullshit that might come their away, and he was double-breasted as always.

TY was the name Run Thang's young go-getter was born with, but "Monsta" was the only name he would answer to. He was a nineteen-year-old country-strong nigga that stood six feet five inches off the ground and tipped the scales somewhere around two-fifty, all solid. Monsta's looks matched his figure to a T, and he was about as cute as Shaq cuddled up with a puppy. His forehead was a mile long over droopy eyes cocked every which way but straight, and it seemed as though his mouth was still filled with baby teeth, all crooked.

Monsta's ugliness wasn't just skin-deep either. He was as mean as he looked and just as dumb. He even misspelled his "wurds" when he "tawk'd," and thinking too hard about anything only got him confused. But none of those qualities had anything to do with how he got his name.

About a year back, TY's younger sister Toya stumbled across his stash of rego in a bedroom drawer, and she let one of her conniving friends talk her into blowing it up in smoke. Of course big bruh was mad as hell, but he understood the traps of peer pressure. Since Toya didn't have the necessary funds to replace the buds, he took it light on lil sis and let her finance the purchase with seven easy payments, and she was preapproved - no credit check. Unfortunately for her, TY wasn't interested in cash. He was only accepting sexual favors - head once a day for a week.

Toya tried her best to honor that debt and get those bills in on time, but he was making her swallow. After the first three installments her stomach couldn't take it anymore. That was when she finally built up enough courage to run and tell their mother. Lucky for her, moms was just as mean and almost as big as her son.

She didn't hesitate to revoke his family membership, and after she got done tossing all his shit out into the hallway, she called him a "monsta," told him to get lost, and then hit him in the ass with the door knob on the way out. Toya was packed up and shipped off to granny's before big bruh could get paid in full.

Either way, TY liked the sound of "monsta" so much he decided to keep it, and it only took him a week or two to get word out that the name change was official. Around that same time was when he first got Run Thang's attention. One day a couple of local thugs, brothers everyone called the Tough Tonies, spotted the youngsta on the ball courts, and they decided to practice some new bully tactics on him. But Monsta wasn't impressed, and evidently they didn't get the memo on his reputation, so he made an example out of the first Tony to run up.

The big youngsta checked the man's chin so hard it changed his "Y" chromosome to an "X"-bully to bitch. The other Tony held his own for a round or two but eventually caught a bad case of whiplash from an uppercut. He was finally choked out in a headlock.

Run Thang happened to be on location scouting for potential, and he drafted the rookie with a first-round pick that guaranteed him a starting spot on the team.

Back in the parking lot, still leaning against the Chevy's grill, Twin logged off of FB, slid his phone into a pocket, and then pulled out a Black & Mild stuffed with some loud, sticky shit. As he put a flame to the tip, a different kind of game drew his attention over to the back entrance of the 30 Block. A couple of young knuckleheads from his crew had cornered a building rat, and they were tag teaming her with a cheap bottle of E&J and some dirt weed. While one of them was sugar coating his lingo with sweet things he thought she wanted to hear, his partner was getting straight to the point and blowing in her ear. "What it do, shawty?"

Run Thang recognized the girl as Robbie, the fifteen-year-old daughter of a local hooker who used to trick for a pimp name Game

Tight until crack stole her glamour. Then hepatitis made her dangerous and just plain worthless.

Robbie was tall for her age, not too cute but curvy with the kind of pooty-booty that made grown men chase it, nothing to brag about though. Her eyes were large and pretty but had their innocence wiped out a long time ago. Evidently she had better taste than what the two young thugs were offering, because they were having a helluva time busting her down.

"Gangsta," Monsta's deep voice rumbled through the muscles of his chest, pulling the twin's attention away from the entertainment at the back door. The big youngsta nodded over to the far end of the lot where a familiar midnight-blue Crown Vic spiked with antennas was headed their way.

The unmarked cruiser stirred up warning shouts of "one time," "heads up," and "slick boys in the lot" from every doorway, window, rooftop, and anywhere else lookouts were posted. Instead of weaving through the mine field of potholes, broken glass, and rusty nails, the Ford hopped a curb and made a shortcut across the grassless dirt until it pulled up behind the box Chevy.

Run Thang passed the burning Black to his young homie, and then they both stepped towards the driver's side tinted window. The glass slid down to reveal a face damn near as black and ugly as Monsta's, with the kind of texture cocoa butter was invented for.

The cop behind the wheel was so well known around that neck of the projects he was called by his first name, Angel. But nothing about the cop fit the typical image of a police officer, and "to protect and serve" wasn't part of his job description either. In Angel's case, it was safe to judge the book by its cover. And just like the old saying "takes one to know one," any crook worth their weight could finger him as one of their own. Angel was a career criminal with a badge, and he and Run had been partners for more than a year already.

"Gangsta," the cop acknowledged the twin with a nod then fixed his stare on Monsta. There was no respect in it.

"If you had any brain cells left, your mind would be a terrible thing to waste." To Angel, the big gorilla was just an overgrown flunky, and he couldn't stand him.

Monsta's buzz from the dro smoke kept him from thinking fast enough to catch the cop's sarcasm, but his instincts had no problem picking up on the negative vibes. To let the undercover dick know the feelings were mutual, he exhaled a gray cloud across his face then smiled in a way only an ugly gorilla could - one that said he didn't give a fuck.

"I should make you suck on that mothafucka." Angel was a ten year vet and intimidation tactics didn't work on him, but Run Thang broke up the petty squabble with a nod that faded his flunky back a few steps.

The twin didn't get it twisted, though. He never exactly saw eye to eye with the detective either, and if it hadn't been for an unusual set of circumstances, fate probably would never had let their paths cross in the first place.

Back when Fool was just kicking off his down state tour of the prison system, Chicago was rolling out a new blueprint for low income housing, and they started by tearing down projects all over the city. Cabrini was at the top of the list for demolition, and wrecking balls took thirty-something buildings down to less than half that. The local mobs were quick to war over what was left, and Run Thang's hustle got hectic fast. That's when the police tried to muscle in on the action, and they set the stage for a pair of gangster mentalities with the same vision to do a collabo.

It was no secret Fool was the twin born with most of the brains, but Run Thang popped out of the pussy holding the muscle, and he had a killer's instincts. He grew up heartless with no conscience, and with a ruthless reputation that made him an alpha dog among mutts. He might not have been a marketing whiz like his brother, but he ran the buildings in Gangsta City with an iron fist. Everybody making a fast buck had to check-in, from the candy man slanging

Now & Laters on the first floor of the Fab 40 to the bootlegger serving up shots at the top of the 30 Block. He would've even had the garbage men kicking in if he could've figured out how to squeeze a buck out of them.

Angel's motivation had always been greed, and his only inspiration was money. He was crooked as crooked got, and he had way more uses for his badge than just fighting crime, like extortion, shakedowns, and hunting down the best drug connects in the city. That's what made their partnership a perfect fit. While Angel plugged them into the pipelines, Run Thang pumped it through his spots, and he kept the soldiers in line, either the easy way or the hard way.

"So what's to those buds?" The cop was quick to get on business. He nodded over at Monsta whose fat lips were wrapped around the Black & Mild.

"Its aight," Run Thang spoke for his flunky. The green was part of a sample Angel sent over for a taste test.

A few days ago, the twin clued-in his partner with some inside info on their competition. The cop chased the lead with a crew of detectives and some bogus warrants, and after kicking down a few doors, they finally located the stash. A brick of Mexican mud, twelve pounds of weed, and a jar of X pills were ready to be delivered.

"Can you move that shit?" Angel was only concerned with one thing.

"Like Geico." Selling weed in Cabrini was so easy even a caveman could do it. Besides, Run Thang could sugarcoat a piece of shit and make it taste like chocolate cake. Plus, his heavy handed tactics already had a lock on three of Gangsta City's buildings— more retail space than a shopping mall—but the greedy cop wanted to be the only one-stop shop in the area, and he was ready to roll back prices even Wal-Mart couldn't beat.

"What about your brother?" Everyone thought Fool was down for the count, stretched out with a life sentence, no parole. Angel was the first to get word on the twin's release, and he didn't want him staking a claim to the same land.

Run Thang shrugged off the question. He tried reaching out to see where Fool's mind was at, but no word came back, and he was starting to think that animosity over the past had something to do with it. He wouldn't lose any sleep over it either way. If Fool stepped outside his body, Run Thang was always ready for combat.

"Problems cause heat..." Angel could read his partner's mind. The detective knew better than to underestimate the other twin. Besides, wars didn't just kill people, they killed profits.

Monsta was reading minds too, and he laughed at the possibilities. He pulled back his shirt at the waist to expose a pair of matching 9's. He named them Ning and Ding.

"Aight," Angel left the subject alone, for the moment, and his thoughts were already shifting to other business. He made quick eye contact with his partner then rerouted the stare over toward Robbie, standing by the back entrance swigging on E&J with the two youngsters still breathing down her neck.

Run Thang read the situation like a crystal ball. Ever since Angel pulled up, he had a feeling the cop was only talking business as a smoke screen. He liked to keep his dirt on the low and only ever popped up in broad daylight for one reason. The twin grabbed back the black from Monsta then whistled to get Robbie's attention. The two knuckleheads didn't bother hiding their disappointment when she spun off of them, but they knew better than to huff and puff about it.

When Robbie walked up, Run Thang used a finger to lift her chin and adjust the focus on her pretty eyes. She parted her lips as if to say something, but he cut her off with the tip of the Black. He dug into a pocket as she pulled, and when her mouth opened slightly to blow out the smoke, he popped in a pill. Then he bent down to blow in her ear.

"You need to shake those D-league niggas and go pro."

Run Thang took a step back and sized her up from head to toe, then back up to her hips. The girl's eyes lit up with a smile, nothing shy about it.

"You're good for a rookie contract, maybe some new kicks and some gear." Run nodded over at his partner, making sure she was on the same page. Robbie's head was already nodding.

"What you want me to do?"

"First, I need you to campaign for the cause," Run Thang sold more dreams than the sandman, and he had the young girl star struck. "I'll take care of you later."

Robbie was sucking on the treat Run gave her as he helped her into the passenger seat. Before he could tell his partner to holla back, the Crown Vic was already shifting into gear.

Angel got what he really came for, and he didn't waste any time peeling rubber out of the parking lot. He bent the wheel with one hand and unzipped his fly with the other. By the time the Ford made it to the end of the lot, he was reaching for the back of Robbie's head.

# Chapter Three

Fool might've spent the last six calendars in the joint working for pennies and peanuts, but at least he came home with a plan to improve his tax bracket.

Most of the twin's time was spent around standard-issue convicts, from killers to thieves and predators to peons. Some were plugged thugs with true stories to share, while others were just knockoff niggas who lied to kick it. Every now and then, a certified heavy would make his presence felt, one who still had juice on the street and connects across the border. The fattest cat of them all was an old Puerto Rican known as Tuffy, chief of a gang that called themselves Spanish Cobras.

The usual prison activities like spades and dominos had Fool and El Jefe rotating in the same social circles, and eventually they grew tight during the occasional brain storming session. Tuffy's motto was "The game don't stop cuz a playa got popped." But "each one-teach one" wasn't part of his economic philosophy. As far as he was concerned, whoever didn't already know didn't need to know, and he definitely wasn't filling in the blanks.

So when word came down on Fool's release, the twin put in his bid with the old man without seeming thirsty for a plug. He knew Tuffy was always looking for opportunities to spread his wings into new markets, and the goldmine in Cabrini was no secret. Plus, Fool's street creds were certified A+, even by the haters.

Tuffy jumped at the opportunity to sponsor Fool's enterprising endeavors. His original offer tapped access to some serious weight and left just enough wiggle room on the prices to give the twin a leg up on his competition, and eventually squeeze them out. Whoever was cashing in on Gangsta City's addicts, Tuffy wanted that paper rerouted into his own pipeline.

That would've been a sweet rookie contract for a first round draft pick, but Fool was a former all-star and league MVP, so he held out for a franchise tag. He talked the old man into keeping the wiggle room on the prices, and giving him enough time to juggle it until he got on his own feet. Once he pumped up his own clientele, Fool promised to push that paper at Tuffy with a forklift.

That's how the deal was done, and on the way out the front gate, El Jefe slid Fool his man's number with instructions to get in touch ASAP. The twin touched down on Cabrini Green's tarmac with a squad of talent ready to shake up the league. All he had to do was order some jerseys and get his team on the court, which was always easier said than done.

When it came to black markets and rackets in the projects, competition was never appreciated and always frowned upon, sometimes with warnings, most times with bullets. And despite Knuck's side of the story, word on the street said Run Thang was the man with the bag, and he had the game in Gangsta City in a strangle hold. While everyone else was pushing match heads for dimes, he was knocking customers in the head with bricks for the same price. He even had profits on heroin fluctuating more wildly than gas prices at the pump, but the fiends were loving the octane.

Fool hadn't figured out yet how his brother managed to orchestrate that takeover, but it was obvious that some heavies were backing it with deep pockets. Still, he recognize the tactics though. One of Fool's old business models was to keep customers off balance by flooding them with new products every couple of weeks. He would introduce a dope line with free samples of a raw batch, no cut, and then give it a catchy name. The first few lucky customer to taste-test it did his word-of-mouth advertising. Soon traffic would start rolling in nonstop around the clock, and that's when he would slowly hit it with shake and bake to blow up the profit margins until he recovered his up-front investment.

Eventually, rumor would get out the bad news, "The bomb turned to bullshit," and the stampede of customers would gradually slow to a crawl. That's when Fool would press the reset button on the operation, open a new line with a different name and more free samples, and then repeat the process all over again. Cluckers and dope fiends have never been the smartest kids in the classroom, and it was easy to keep them spinning in circles from one okee-doke to the next. Some of Fool's top sellers were Asswipe, Bitch Slap, and Sucka Punch. At the moment, Run Thang was over in the 30 Block recycling those same old tricks with dope lines called Anti-up and Game Over.

As far as Fool was concerned, he was done playing games for those peanuts. There were too many hustlers in the suburbs and small towns around Chicago who were long on customers but short on supply. Instead of setting up shop in the projects with shelves stacked with product, he was switching his business model over to wholesaling and distribution. He could stack just as many chips with less traffic by charging niggas a toll to ride his connects. And he could duck most of the heat by setting up on and off ramps like obstacle courses between him and his clientele. Flunkies would handle the routes and jump through the hurdles while he worked dispatch.

To Fool, "Gangster" wasn't just a word, it was a way of life, and "money by any means" was the only way to live it. The twin was a G by birth, down since baby steps and googoo gahgah. But in the real gangland of Cabrini, jump-ins were for peons, and niggas only got OG status in the movies. Loyalty was all about who could feed who, and lucky for Fool, Knuck had kept his own team fat while he was gone. And they were all itching to get back at Run Thang for trying to stunt their growth.

Another concept of "Gangster" Fool liked to subscribe to was using stunt dummies to do his dirty work. Instead of putting his own team on the front-lines, he would rather push the local addicts into play, and he'd masterminded the strategy of sacrificing pawns a long time ago.

Crack heads and dope fiends crawled he streets day and night like rats and roaches scavenging for crumbs to stuff pipes or jab into veins. And no matter the habit, the hustles were all the same, and there were no days off when the monkey had to be fed. Whether boosting from stores, snatching purses, or breaking into parking meters for change, a junky would work his fingers to the bone for a fix. But instead of knocking old ladies off their canes for a few dollars, Fool was ready to offer them an opportunity to earn an honest buck. He was the local day-labor for addicts, and his gigs were guaranteed. All they had to do was show up, and if one of them happened to get popped for distribution of a controlled substance, "Better you than me" would be written in the fine print of their hiring papers. Besides, there were always hungry hypes willing to step into those boots and take that spot on the frontline.

Early that morning, Fool and Knuck posted "Help wanted" signs around the projects, and before they were back in their office, the Carter was packed with potential employees lined up with applications in hand and ready to punch a clock. But the crowd was too thick, and Fool didn't want to waste time on that many interviews, so his first order of business was weeding through the candidates who had a little too much going on with themselves to be usable.

A prime example was an old-head whose face was covered in so many infected bumps and blisters that he looked ready to explode in a bomb of green and yellow puss. Nobody could really remember his name, but he had been haunting the projects so long everyone got used to calling him Ghost.

Then there were the mental patients and retarded dummies who couldn't get right no matter what, or take orders for shit. Fool definitely wasn't sweating the cost of health insurance, but there was no way in hell he was going to let a bunch of zombies and nutcases scare away his business. The final contestants were narrowed down to a handful of vets, battle tested but not shell shocked. A few more were told to stay tuned in case the first crew didn't last long. Of course the twin would keep the team of Gangstas on security duty, making sure the runners didn't get stuck by any stickup men, or try to pull a Houdini, pop smoke and disappear.

With his vendor on speed dial, and after Tuffy quoted the prices, Fool calculated his point spread just enough to keep everybody eating without gouging the mark-up too much. Then, all he had to do was get the word out about the grand opening, sit back, and wait for his phone to cha-ching like a cash register.

Duke

# Chapter Four

It was all-star weekend in Gangsta City, and ballers from all over the projects were pounding the courts with And 1 crossovers and Lob City hops, and only the top vote getters were getting any of the playing time.

But the homegrown ballers weren't showing off their skills for talent scouts offering scholarships, and the tournaments weren't for trophies or awards either. The day's competition was sponsored by the hustlers and Gangstas who were also setting the odds and writing the contracts. Lucky for the house, the bleachers were packed, standing room only, and all bets were booked solid.

The basketball stars weren't the only players making highlights though. A-listers from other neighborhoods mingled on the sidelines stunting hard in new gear, G'd up and jeweled out. Chicks with cute faces and thick thighs played their groupie roles, while the wanna-be's acted like their paparazzi. Court-side was strictly reserved for attention seekers. Broke niggas and flat asses stood shy at the back of the crowd.

Of course, the local celebs wouldn't be out-done on their home court. Run Thang was the defending champ, and the man every baller worth his weight was gunning for. Four summers and running, the twin held down the title of number one stunna, undisputed, and he was quick to bust a nigga's dick in the dirt with the size of a bet or crush a sucka's ego by snatching his bitch. He even parked his Beamer on the edge of the sidelines, blacked-out and sitting low on rims that kissed the concrete with chrome lips. His overgrown protégé rode shotgun, reclining on ox blood leather and soaking up the A/C.

The weekend event also had an old fan favorite in attendance. Word was out that Fool beat his murder rap, and the crowd was thick with people who wanted to rub shoulders with the former MVP. While the real niggas congratulated, fake ones hated, and a handful who had the inside scoop knew it was the first time the twins would cross paths in six years, and they wanted to see if tension would turn to friction.

Fool wasn't there to entertain his fans though, and he wasn't in on the tournaments either. His game plan was "Now you see me-now you don't," and he left the betting for the suckers. As he navigated through the gangstas and prankstas crowding the courts, the only stunting he did was with Tameeka looking gorgeous under his arm, done up in a sexy little package of tight shorts and a cut-off T. She picked the fit herself to show off her curvy chocolate, while Fool took care of the other details like her hair and nails.

A week after cutting the ribbon on his grand opening, Fool had been taking more orders than a McDonalds drive-thru on lunch break. Just the other day, he flipped a new whip, an old-school Caddy dipped in candy with a gold grill, and he had it gassed up to take baby girl for a day out of the hood, somewhere on the lake front, then maybe a cross-border trip to one of the casinos over in Indiana. Later, his plans included swinging Tameeka by a two-bedroom rental he recently copped on the Northside, and then pealing the wrapper off of a new king-sized mattress for a proper break-in.

On the opposite end of the court from Fool and Tameeka, Run Thang sat mean-mugging through the tints of his Beamer with thoughts of jealousy. Seeing his twin with the sexy star riding his hip reminded him of how they fell out in the first place. He knew Fool would wait until he was back on top of his game before he started mingling in crowds, and Run Thang was feeling his presence like a black cloud of hate hanging over that old grudge. He reached over and tapped Monsta on the shoulder.

"What you think about that nigga's bitch?"

The look on the flunky's face exposed his thoughts before he could get the words out, mouth stuck open like a fly trap with a cockeyed stare pointed in their direction.

"Dats a baad lil muh fuka." Eyeballing Tameeka gave Monsta an instant craving for chocolate.

Run Thang spotted a small group of youngsters standing a few feet behind the cute couple, and they were all caught up in Fool's stardom just like everyone else, as if the future hood hall-of-famer was about to start signing autographs. One of Cabini's oddest residents stuck out of the crowd like a sore thumb, but looking less star struck and more like he was mesmerized by the shake of Tameeka's hips. He was a young teenage boy who drew attention everywhere he went, but definitely not the flattering kind.

No one really knew what name the kid was born with, but "Creep" was the only one he went by in the projects. He was a retard with looks to match – as if an evil witch had cast a spell that turned him into a little troll. Another mystery about the boy, besides how his brain got turned around backwards, was his age, since he never learned how to count past his fingers and toes, and he lost track of his birthdays a few years ago.

In spite of the unsolved mysteries, some of the more popular rumor's about the boy's circumstances were either he got ahold of his mom's crack pipe when he was little, or she was putting more than just formula in his baby bottle. Either way, Creep's brain cells started backfiring sometime around kindergarten, and he had never been able to think straight since. But the boy wasn't completely fucked up like everyone believed. He was only about three-fourth retarded, and his view of the world was only slightly twisted. Whenever he blanked-out, it was only a part-time trip, sort of like a sherm head popping an occasional mushroom.

Life certainly hadn't been too kind to Creep, and he could always be spotted wearing the same rags and kicks whenever he snuck into a game: a pair of ball-busting shorts, a tattered jersey he found in a dumpster behind a school, and some chucks he transformed into Mikes with a red maker.

Run Thang couldn't have cared less what the retard's real name was, and he damn sure didn't give a fuck about his true story, but he did know all about the boy's rep and how he liked to touch himself while peeping through windows at night. Run also knew that Creep's mentality was about as unstable as a suicide bomber's with a lit stick of dynamite, and the way his attention was locked on Fool's bitch at the moment gave the twin an idea how he could take advantage of the little pervert and his freaky urges.

As Run Thang's thoughts were switching from jealousy to plans for revenge, Monsta noticed a newcomer to Cabrini's tournaments hanging out on the sidelines. It was the suburban chick who dumped the back-shots on Run's Facebook. The flunky wasted no time pointing her out.

A mixed complexion and long frizzy curls with auburn highlights, all natural, made her easy to spot in the crowd. Her body type was tall and slim, with the kind of curves that had a swarm of wanna-be's buzzing around as if she were a flower, and they were spitting their lingo in her ear for the honey. But the cutie wasn't falling for the bullshit though, and when Run Thang tapped his horn to get her attention, she shook off the buzzards and made a b-line for the Beamer.

The tinted windows slid down and the twin leaned out for a clearer view of her walk. He was definitely digging the way she ripped the runway. Run couldn't remember her name, but no matter, he knew what he was going to call her anyway.

"Red, you like that attention?"

The cutie smiled, not shyly, but with the kind of confidence that said she knew what she was working with, and exactly how to use it.

"All they see is this hair and these hips."

"And lips," Run Thang was digging her sexiness, too.

"And ass," and so was Monsta.

"I was just check'n out those pics." The twin kept Red smiling.

"You like?" She did a half-spin then leaned on it with a Next Top Model pose. She got the right reaction with an "Ooh wee" from the driver's side, and a "God damn" from the passenger seat.

Run Thang reached out and palmed the bottom curve of her ass with a squeeze. It was his favorite body part, and hers was even softer than he imagined. The pleasant surprise made him lick his greedy kips.

"The projects sho don't make'em like the suburbs." He sized up the rest of her before asking, "You pop?"

"Got pills?" The glassy gleam in Red's pretty brown eyes told Run that she was already swerving.

"Like Walgreens." The twin clicked the door locks, and Red climbed into the backseat.

Run Thang didn't waste any time putting the old grudge against Fool on hold, along with his plan for revenge. Figuring out how to send the retarded Creep off on a mission was going to be easy, and he could always iron out the details later. At the moment, Red had his freak cranked to the max, and he was fiending to find out what kind of tricks she would turn for a treat.

Duke

# Chapter Five

When Fool went shopping for a whip, he took a trip back to the early 70's and copped a big-body Caddy, four doors with a rag on the top. He kept the theme pimpin' with a dip in red candy-apple jam and down-graded the 22's for a set of throwback thirty-spokes wrapped in vogues.

Tameeka wasn't feeling the look at first, but when the back of her thighs hit the crushed-velvet on the pillow seats, it didn't take her long to start digging that old-school flavor.

Just like the brougham, Fool put a lot of thought into their trip out of the hood, but his cards didn't fall exactly the way he stacked them. The day began with the forecast calling for partly cloudy skies and cool breezes, so he kicked off their date at North Avenue beach. Unfortunately, the weatherman couldn't predict the crowds of parents showing up with their kids, and Fool got a good fifteen minutes of tossing Tameeka around in the water before they had to put their clothes back on and keep their fun rated-G for the viewing audience. Luckily, a light drizzle gave him an excuse to cut short that boring entertainment before it got too stale.

They packed up the picnic basket, shook off the sand, and hopped back into the whip for a run across the Indiana border. A club at one of the casinos advertised a stand-up, a nerdy white dude making his debut to the stage, but half-way through the act shit got wack. So, the couple decided to try their luck on the craps table, and then a few hands of blackjack, but it didn't take long to see their chips weren't stacking up right and that made Fool go back to the drawing board for a date saver.

The twin figured a little shopping would put the day back on track with no problem. On the way back north, he took her to a downtown boutique to pick a few fits, and he even decorated her neck and wrist with a little color. Normally, Fool only fed carats to rabbits, but Tameeka was down when his feet were just getting off the ground, so he didn't mind giving her a return on her investment. Besides, he wouldn't be a proper D-boy if his girl couldn't stunt on her friends with something to brag about.

By the time Fool's pockets were getting tapped out, the sun was making its exit west as the day got later, so they jumped back on the e-way headed north towards his new digs to wind down the evening with a nightcap.

Bucktown was where Fool found his two-bedroom flat. It sat in a mostly mixed middle class neighborhood, with green grass and the kind of peace and quiet that required a clean background and top-flight credit just to qualify for a studio apartment. Luckily, he was able to duck that microscope when he got plugged with a landlord who was also a pervert that liked to tweak. Hooking him up with a young trick was the lease agreement, powdering his nose was the first month's rent and security deposit.

Tameeka was impressed when Fool pulled up in front of the four-story gray-stone and backed the Caddy's big body into a tight parking spot.

"Why you move all the way out here?" To her, the neighborhood was like leaving the ghetto for Hollywood, and the lack of black faces made her uncomfortable.

"Laying my head where I do my dirt is like shitting in my own backyard." Plus, Fool didn't have to duck bullets all day, and he liked being able to let his guard down once in a while.

As he grabbed the shopping bags full of goodies from the back seat, Tameeka had more questions.

"How much? A lot?" The building looked like it would take half a year of her public aid checks for one month's rent.

"Not for real," he left out the details as he ushered her inside.

Earlier, Fool debated whether or not to even let her know about his new digs. Fuck-buddies usually got the motel treatment anyway. From past experience, he knew when narcs launched their investigations, girlfriends were always their first target. And when they tightened the screws, the pressure would make most women bust and reveal the location of their nigga's honeycomb hideout. And even though they had been hitting it off pretty well, Tameeka was the one who laid down the rules of engagement. She wasn't expecting to be wifed.

Well, Fool wasn't looking for a live-in either. He knew how to keep a leash on his feelings. Besides, his new apartment was only temporary. So, in the meantime, there was nothing wrong with pretending they were on a honeymoon. He even intended on raw-dogging her, no more rubbers.

In the second-floor hallway, Fool jiggled his keys for a few seconds, which was an old habit. In the projects, he kept a pair of blood-thirsty pits roaming loose inside his safe house, and they would go nuts if he walked in without giving then a heads-up. But in his new neck of the woods, guard dogs were a no-no, and the neighbors would be the one's going nuts.

Inside, Fool flicked on the lights and dropped the shopping bags by the door. Even though the two-bed, one and a half bathroom was kind of heavy on his wallet, he didn't really cop the apartment to impress anybody. He kept the remodel conservative, light on the leather, wood, and electronics. Instead, he used his spare cash to splurge on necessities like a few built in hiding spots for his guns and money.

Fool took Tameeka over to a fish tank he had set up between the kitchen and front room. He hit a switch that lit fifty-five gallons of water and a pair of red bellied piranhas the size of small frying pans with sharp teeth.

Fool tapped on the glass and Tameeka "oohed" at the pretty pets. Like his girl, the twin enjoyed treating his pets to the finer things in life, and he spoiled his fish with a sunken sailboat, a treasure chest overflowing with fake gold, and a naked mermaid with perky breasts and hard pink nipples. Earlier that morning, he stopped by a mom and pop pet shop to pick up their breakfast; two bug-eyed goldfish, and a handful of guppies. Fool also liked a little entertainment when he fed his killer fish. He enjoyed watching them chase around their food.

The goldfish were fat and clumsy swimmers, but if they were eaten first, the piranhas would be too full and slow to catch up with the lightning fast guppies. So, instead of dunking their meal in all at once, Fool left the goldfish inside the sandwich bag he brought them in and let them float at the top of the tank to watch their little buddies get served up like appetizers. At the moment, all that was left were crumbs, and the piranhas were burning off some of the calories swimming slow circles around their main course.

"Can't you feed'em some hamburger meat or something?" Tameeka was kind of creeped-out by the thought of the goldfish being eaten alive.

"Ain't nothing but a couple fish." Fool never thought of goldfish as anything other than dinner for bigger fish.

"But that one's look'n at me." One of the bug-eyed goldfish was moving its lips as if it was trying to say, "This is some bullshit."

That got a laugh from Fool. He didn't want to tease his pets any longer than he had to, but he didn't want to get Tameeka grossed-out, and he damn sure wasn't going to spoil her mood. He flipped the script to keep things playful by snatching her close and zeroing in on her lips with his, but he pulled up short at the last second.

"Ready for the grand tour?" He started leaning her in the direction of the bedroom, but Tameeka hip-checked him before he could finish the move.

"VIP?" she started grinding his thigh like a kitty begging to be stroked.

Fool didn't need an interpreter to read Tameeka's body language, and besides, he picked the lock on her orgasms his first night home, and he had been busting her open on a regular every night since.

Fool knew exactly how to tickle Tameeka's turn-ons; confidence, something spontaneous, and she liked to get it pounded, the rougher the better. At first, Fool hesitated on that last part. He was scared to damage the pussy. But since he gave as well as he took, he was beating her pussy up in no time.

Tameeka didn't want any mercy that night either, and she didn't waste any time getting things cracking. She slipped out of her shirt and stepped through her shorts, no panties or bra for easy access. Fool followed her lead and his shirt went flying off to the left, jumpers kicked into a corner, and before they could make it out of the front room, his jeans were already somewhere on the floor behind him, commando, no undies.

Fool kept their chemistry percolating with a tongue down her throat, and he smothered her body from all angles at once—breasts, waist, ass, and thighs—as if he had eight arms and sixteen hands.

Tameeka showed off some of her own skills, stroking his dick until he was stiff as a soldier standing at attention. She honored his drill sergeant with a salute, *ten hut*, then grabbed him around his neck and jumped up into his arms. She clamped her legs around his waist tighter than a pair of vise grips, and her fingernails dug into his back like hooks.

"Been wait'n on this dick all day," Tameeka's voice oozed like syrup in Fool's ear, warm and sweet. "And it's been a looong day."

"That kitty fiend'n for a hit?" He tickled her with his soldier.

"Like catnip." Tameeka loved the dirty talk.

Fool took that as his cue, and he responded with more aggressiveness than a fighter coming out of his corner, round one. He slammed her back against the nearest wall, and every muscle from his calves to his hips strained to punch on her pussy.

"Hmm," Tameeka loved being his punching bag. "Hit it with a combo."

Fool unwound with a right-left-right.

"Umm," she begged him to beat her up. "Uppercut it."

Fool's jabs, hooks, and haymakers had her pussy on the ropes, and he pounded on her sexy body until he heard the drywall cracking. Luckily for his security deposit, Fool could fuck while he walked, and he fucked her all the way into the bedroom. He only paused his gymnastics long enough to toss her on the bed.

Tameeka stuck the landing with a perfect ten, back arched and legs spread just right. She reached down with one hand and split it with a middle finger.

"Damn, gurl, that's sexy as hell." Her performance had Fool's mouthwatering.

"Come get it," she struck a pose with a look that told him he was still in control of her body, and she wanted him to ride it like his old-school caddy.

Fool didn't hesitate a second. He jumped behind the wheel, strapped her legs over his shoulders like seatbelts, and then mashed on the gas until he had her little engine revving like a V-8. He adjusted Tameeka's throttle with his penetration, and when her tach started hitting the red-line, thighs vibrating just right, he popped her clutch and took her for a spin around the king-sized mattress.

Fool pounded on it for a few laps, missionary, and Tameeka pounded right back. Then they flipped positions and she took over the wheel, whipping it like she was bending corners doing sixty miles per hour. But her speed was a little too much for the twin and his own motor started to overheat, damn near about to blow a head gasket. But he wasn't ready to quit the race just yet, and he lifted her up so he could slide out for a breather. He needed to let his radiator cool off for a few seconds.

Tameeka knew he wasn't teasing, though, just a stall tactic. While he caught his breath, she helped keep his libido stiff by flipping over, stomach down, ass up.

The quick pit stop did the trick and had his tank feeling topped-off. He mashed back on the gas and rear-ended her harder than a Suburban breaking the speed limit with no brakes. Tameeka's first instincts made her run from the collision, but Fool's reaction times were too fast, and he chased her ass across the bed until he had her cornered at the headboard. He reached around the front until his fingers found her pink bundle of nerves, and then he plucked it like a guitar string.

But Fool couldn't play the whole band by himself, and he needed to get back on his own instrument, drums, so he pulled one of her hands down to help him finish the song. And in case she forgot the words, he whispered the lyrics in her ear. "Make that pussy cum."

Tameeka's body shuddered when he got back on the bass. Fool beat on it, grinding and digging deep. It didn't take long before she finally let go, and her contractions were grabbing and pulling him in even deeper. Her climax created a wave of heated tension that threatened to bust between Fool's legs. But instead of letting it blow, he pulled out again for another stall tactic. He slid to the edge of the bed and put the pin back in his grenade.

Tameeka wasn't having it that time and she crawled over on all fours to catch him while his throbbing was still strong. Fool's muscles tensed when she wrapped her sexy lips around the head of his dick. She took her time, teeth munching softly, sucking him down one slow inch at a time. Her lip-slurping and head-bobbing dick tricks had the twin's eyes rolling to the back of his head and he struggled to stay focused. He wasn't going to miss that show for nothing in the world.

After a few rounds of palm friction, Tameeka's deep-throat finally got Fool's throbbing cranked to the max, heads-up for what was about to come. At the last second, she pulled back up to his tip and munched down with more pressure from her teeth, super head.

Fool felt his energy draining with every squirt. To an amateur, it would've seemed as though he was just another two minute brother with no stamina. But just as Tameeka gave him the combo to her lock, he taught her the ancient art of keeping a Mandingo warrior on some Zulu shit all night.

After Tameeka swallowed, she shifted gears and dialed up the suction on her mouth. Hands, tongue, and teeth, she handled her tools like a mechanic and had him back up and running in no time. Then she took her position at the starting line, back arched and thighs cocked. To tease him in her direction, she used her middle finger to crack another sexy smile.

# Chapter Six

While Fool was in Bucktown TKO'ing Tameeka in the last round, his twin was across town club hopping through the south side mobbed-deep with his crew out of the 30 Block. By the time night started turning into morning, Run Thang was headed back to Cabrini, Monsta still riding sidekick in the scrub seat, and cutie Red x-ed out in the back and trying to hold her liquor.

As they were pulling into the lot, Angel was just coming off an all-nighter with Robbie, and he returned her with only a little wear and tear, no repairs needed. Since shorty was showing so much dedication, Run Thang gave her an invitation to his after party.

The twin kept a pad on the top floor of the Fab 40 that he called the Groupie Lounge, and he had the project penthouse decked out like a sex palace with more freaky shit than the Bunny Ranch in Vegas. Mirrors clung to the ceilings, flat screens hung from all the walls, and video cameras were posted in the corners ready to catch all the action from every angle in HD.

Run Thang mostly used the spot to turn out new talent, and he often found himself mixed up in more ménage a tois` than a French porno star. Busting two sluts down with no jealousy was no challenge for a P like him. And before he could pop the top off a pill bottle, he had his Lay-Z-Boy kicked back in the V.I.P. section with Red and Robbie on the floor between his legs passing his dick back and forth while he snapped pics with his phone. Fool might be able to fuck while he walked, but Run could bash in two brains, post the pics on Facebook and update his status at the same damn time.

The caption on the twin's latest upload read, "A playa in his leisure time." Feedback from his friends' list was getting posted on his wall as fast as their fingers could tap their touchscreens.

GI: Redbone is a STUNNA!!!
Murda: But whos da booga?
LowEnd: She sooo ugly its SEXY!

Run: She got skills tooo! Watch dis...

RunThang handed the phone to Red with a few quick directions for the photo shoot. Robbie had her extensions tied back in a pair of schoolgirl pigtails. Run grabbed them like handlebars and jabbed the back of her throat until her gag reflex began to spasm and she started choking out sound effects.

"Uck-Ack-Uck..."

Robbie's tonsils popped like a clutch, but she hung in tight, and her motor never lost suction.

"Damn, baby gurl, you got potential." Run let the girl up for air when her eyes started to water.

"You like how I'm suck'n this dick?" Robbie knew just what to say and exactly how to say it. She looked up and batted her eyelashes, another pro-move.

Run blew her a kiss right before he stuffed her throat again.

"Uck-Ack-Uck..."

"You wanna start'n spot on a nigga's team?" He pulled back again, and that time she drug her teeth all the way to the tip slurping up every inch along the way.

"Any position?" She munched playfully on the head.

"As long as you share that ball," he nodded over at Monsta lounging in his usual spot by the door, already warmed up off a molly bomb and waiting for coach to put him in the game.

Robbie hesitated. She knew she had an ass like a donkey, but she had a feeling that getting fucked by that nigga would be like getting kicked by a mule. Besides, she was really looking forward to making Run cum.

The girl's bottom lip pouted in disappointment, but she stood up anyway. The twin gave her plump ass a good smack for motivation then took the phone back from Red and slid back into her warm mouth before his dick got cold. The wall on his Facebook was updating faster than a scoreboard at a season opener.

GI: Dammm, shawty can go deep!!!

TreyNine: Gills like a fish-no air!

079: What her stats look like?

Run: Self-esteem-low, Ambition – No, References – Every dick in da hood.

Monsta didn't waste any time putting his own points on the board, and Run snapped a couple quick shots of his flunky trying to poke Robbie in every hole on her body. The scene looked like something out of a scary movie – a giant troll raping a cabbage patch doll. Run zoomed in for a close-up.

GI: Dats a BIG NIGGA!!!

LoEnd: Makn a mess outta da pussy!

Murda: She takn it like a champ tho!

For a minute, Run Thang almost felt sorry for the young rookie, but Robbie's resume was typical hood rat, and being able to take a yard of dick was the minimum qualification for that position. The twin knew all it would take was a small taste of the good life to get her signing on the dotted line and handing over all the rights to that ass.

Sizing up cutie Red was only a little more complicated. She kept her fashion up-to-date and was already used to having her needs spoiled with attention. Plus, she could talk a nigga's ears off, something Run didn't find out until he started popping pills in her mouth. The only way he could shut her the fuck up was by keeping her throat stuffed. Thankfully for the twin's patience, Red was a boss freak with an oral fixation, and when she tweaked off of X, sucking dick was her fetish.

Run Thang quickly figured out the key to lowering the suburban cutie's standards, keeping her prescription filled. Most people would classify her type as "High maintenance," but he just called them "Gas guzzlers" and he could always afford the price at the pump. If Red wanted to stay high, as long as she kept her legs cocked and mouth open, he would keep her flying higher than a pelican.

Run Thang's camera snapped a tight shot of Red's action. He pulled out to give her a breather, and the tip of his dick was oozing nut.

"Mmm," Red sipped on his swilla like a Pina colada. Then she slid him back in her mouth.

Run's Facebook lit up again, and everyone was commenting on the girl's performance.

Murda: That's a baad Bitch!

079: Tha face is a munny'maka!

GI: Take her to da track…

LowEnd: She a runna? Get her sum runnin shoes!

Run: Bout to give her a quick makeover…

Trey Nine: Spa treatment?

Run: Facial…

Run Thang scrolled through his phone's camera option for some special effects. Just as his dick started throbbing in Red's mouth, he zoomed in for another close up. Then he pulled out and blasted off in 3-D, no glasses.

# Chapter Seven

Tameeka had Fool nutting all night, and she didn't stop until she knocked off every nut from the tree. The twin woke up the next morning with his back feeling flimsy as spaghetti, knees squishy like jelly doughnuts. After taking baby girl to scoop mini-me, then dropping them both off on the south side at her mom's, Fool pulled into a gas station/carwash with a built in McDonalds. He needed to top-off the whip and refuel his body.

He sat in a booth by a window smashing breakfast burritos and guzzling coffee, black with six sugars. He used the extra kick in the caffeine to focus. That's how he flipped the switch from weekend boyfriend back to everyday hustler.

Fool scrolled through his phone checking messages. His inbox was packed with overdue orders, but getting them filled wasn't as easy as hitting a "purchase" button like on eBay, and he hadn't figured out how to take debit cards yet like Amazon either.

In the first message Knuck sent word the cops nabbed one of the runners with a small bundle going to one of the spots. Fool tapped out a reply to see who put that deduction on his balance sheet, because losses like that never got written off.

Fool: ???

Knuck: Pooky Slim. He hold'n his weight tho.

Slim wasn't just a temp. He was one of the crew, and the dicks at the station were probably putting the squeeze on him right at that moment. That's why Fool always kept his left hand from knowing what the right hand was doing, and Slim only knew what he was told. Even though there was no honor among thieves, there was still loyalty between G's.

Fool: Manage that bond, ASAP.

Knuck: No doubt. And twin tryna reach out?

Fool: It's tite on that nigga.

Run Thang had been trying to get in touch through Cuz ever since Fool first touched down. Twin was asking questions, throwing his line in the water and fishing for information. The standard operating procedure in Cabrini was monkey see, monkey do, and everyone followed the lead of the most successful. But when one of the monkeys couldn't keep up, the monkeys went to war. That's why Fool kept his playbook classified top-secret, and no way was his brother getting clearance for his phone number. There was no war between the twins, yet, but there was no peace treaty either.

Next on Fool's morning agenda was getting back with one of the Gangstas next door in 714 West Division, the Goldmine. He was a twenty-year nigga who used to rotate in both of the twins' circles. Back in those days, he was known as the "cook" for his reputation of whipping up recipes in the kitchen. With a bowl, some ice water, and a hand-held blender, he could fluff up a half until it looked like a brick, no need to overdose it with B-12 or kill it with too much soda. His chef skills were so crucial he could've had his own show on the Food Network. Now everyone called him WahLah.

Fool was already familiar with those old recipes, and their conversation wasn't about baking that kind of bread. WahLah had been hearing about the octane of the diesel fluid the twin was pushing, and he wanted to add that specialty to his own mean. When they ran into each other a few days ago, Fool slid him his number. The gangsta didn't waste any time getting back with a business model. He proposed introducing value meals – raw tenths for ten dollars. If they kept it simple without getting greedy, there would be no reason to waste money promoting it with gimmicks.

The old cook's plan for pushing only raw heroin was a good marketing tactic for getting Run Thang's customers to switch their brand loyalty, so long as Fool could hold down the prices just enough to make the new product line profitable. The big boys at Wal-Mart and Sam's Club figured that shit out a long time ago.

They didn't operate by squeezing every penny out of a profit. Instead, they moved billons of pennies every day.

Fool was always making moves to stay one step ahead of his competition, and he had been thinking franchise from day one. About a week ago, he rounded up a bunch of local addicts and sent them shopping in Run Thang's building so he could do some product research. The survey said that shit was just average, nothing special, but the quantity was keeping his doors open.

Fool knew the best way to beat quantity was with quality, and as far as he was concerned, the customer was always right. He tapped out the good news to WahLah.

Fool: Whts tha ticket?

WahLah: Wht it hit fo?

Fool: How bad u want it?

WahLah: Tlk $ over lunch

Fool: Bet

The twin's inbox was flooded with more orders, and the supply side of his operation wasn't having any problems filling them.

Tuffy had recently sent word through Loco that his connects across the border were running through mules faster than they could strap on saddlebags. They needed Fool to round up some bitches willing to take trips, swallow balloons, and pack pussies. The old P.R. was proposing to upgrade his membership status from gold to platinum, and with the price discounts to match.

No doubt Fool could make that happen, and he already had Knuck posting more help wanted signs and taking applications. Later, they'd open up the office in 660 and conduct some more interviews. He told Loco to get back with him in a week or so, once he narrowed down the candidates.

Fool tossed the burrito wrappers and took his cup back to the counter for a refill. He added a couple warm cinnabuns to the order, and as he peeled off a dub for the cashier, he overheard a woman at the next counter ordering the same thing. Instinct made him glance over in her direction, but she was facing the other way and he could only get a side angle with a quarter of a back-shot. Nevertheless, it was just enough to turn his sneak peek into a head to toe critique.

The woman couldn't have been standing any taller than five-five, with a figure that had more shape than a video model. But she had it wrapped in a suit, black and silver pinstripes, as if she stepped off the set of Law & Order. Her long hair was streaked with strawberry highlights, tied back and rolled up like she meant business. Fool still couldn't get a 20/20 on her face, but an exotic complexion told a short story of tropical islands, maybe even a little jungle fever.

The cashier slid her coffee across the counter, and then spun off to get a pair of cinnabuns. The lady popped the cup's top, stirred the sugar off the bottom, and then lifted the coffee for a taste test. The movement was just enough to change the angle, and Fool took full advantage of the view. Like a thief returning to the scene of the crime, he redid his critique, letting his eyes drop to size her up properly, from a pair of black patent leather pumps and past thighs thick enough to make a gay nigga go straight and a straight bitch curious. In fact, her look was so gorgeous, Fool would've had a hard time describing it, even if he knew every word in the dictionary.

On his route back past her hips was when she finally caught him staring, and the twin couldn't help feeling like a kid with his hand caught in a cookie jar.

"You want me to strike a pose?" The woman's lips creased in a tight smile that took just enough of the edge off of her sarcasm to make it playful. Then she turned half-way around and paused like she hit the end of a runway at a fashion show.

"Damn," Fool wasn't easily impressed by cute faces, and his improv skills were usually on time, but the confidence of her sex appeal almost made him speechless, almost.

"I didn't mean to lose my composure like that. But since you caught me peek'n, mind if I get my money's worth?"

His reply cracked open her smile, flashing perfect teeth, pearly as the side of a Colgate box, and her light brown eyes told him she appreciated the attention. Fool tried not to expose what his imagination was thinking, but the sassy stranger turned out to be a mind reader

"If you want to spit something slick at me, make it quick, because I have to punch a clock in ten minutes." Not only was her voice sweet, with the kind of raspy note that needed to be on a mic in a studio, but she also used her body language for emphasis. Her hips were quotation marks.

The rest of their orders got dropped on the counter at the same time. The sexy woman looked away long enough to grab hers, then she took the few steps between them and glanced up with a look that expected not to be disappointed.

But that was when Fool caught a glimpse of a badge clipped to the belt on her waist, and it made him rethink what he was about to say. Instead, he asked, "Please tell me that says Top Flight Security?"

Normally, Fool's reaction times were quick to jump at opportunities, but something about the situation felt sticky, and it was slowing his reflexes. His frown even threw her off balance.

"Nope, police, but does it really make a difference?" She seemed to soften her approach to take his guard down a notch, and it worked.

"Naw, makes no difference to me. Name's D'mico." He didn't reach out a hand, since both of theirs were full, but she took his lead anyway.

"Sundae," cute dimples winked as the smile returned to her face. Then she reminded him, "I have to punch that clock, but we can finish our introduction over lunch."

Duke

# Chapter Eight

For Creep the retard, hard knocks was the only way of life, and just about every day was a constant struggle for survival. For him, good days came few and far between, but the sun shines even on a dog's ass every once in a while, and that day, he was having the time of his life.

Earlier that morning, while on one of his dumpster diving adventures through a rich white neighborhood on the Gold Coast, he bumped into a one-eyed stray dog wandering loose in an alley. The retard usually only found stuff like broken toys, tossed out clothes, and occasional snacks. Finding the mutt was almost like hitting the lottery, and he could hardly believe his luck.

Creep decided to call his new buddy "Dead Eye," since he didn't know what else to call it. In fact, he couldn't even figure out if it was a girl or boy, since he had no clue where to look or what to look for. But sometime in his past, Creep vaguely remembered someone telling him that all dogs were boys, and cats girls, so that was good enough for him.

The new friends spent the rest of the afternoon getting to know each other while treasure hunting through people's garbage. After splitting a tuna casserole they found wrapped in aluminum foil, they seemed to form a permanent bond. He couldn't wait to introduce his new best friend to the neighborhood!

Back in the projects, the retard tied Dead Eye to a fence behind his building while he made a run to the corner store for a pack of Twinkies. He had found some loose change in the ashtray of an unlocked car, and he planned to use it on a meal to celebrate his new friendship.

Skipping down the street with pennies, nickels, and dimes jingling in his pockets, Creep was having the time of his life. He pulled up to the crowded store across the street from one of the Wild

End Buildings, 1015-1017, the "Boulevard." He walked inside singing one of his favorite cartoon soundtracks from the Flintstones.

"There's a town I know and a place I go called Bed Rock, twist twist..." Before the door could close behind him, a loud rumble of taunts and teases started flying at him from every direction.

"Get yo filthy ass outta here," someone yelled.

"And take yo lil sista's shirt off," another voice bellowed out.

Someone in the background sized it up as "extra-medium."

A young boy standing next to his mother laughed and pointed at the silver duct tape and Elmer's glue holding the soles to the bottoms of Creep's "Air Gordon's."

"You smell like ass and stink bomb smoke." By then, every face in the store was laughing at him.

"Sticks and stones," Creep shouted back with more confidence than he usually had.

The boy rushed up to the bullet-proof window and tossed a handful of dirty change in the money tray. The man behind the register, an old Vietnamese, was the owner and had been there since the 70's. He always felt sorry for the unfortunate kid and let him butt to the front of the line whenever he came in.

Creep nodded at a row of two-for-a-dollar Twinkies hanging in between boxes of single Swishers and a rack of knock-off Fitted New Eras. The old man knew the boy wanted to make a fast getaway, so he quickly slid his order under the window without counting every penny. Creep spun off as quickly as he could. But on the way back to the door, someone stuck out a foot and tried to trip him.

"Dirty lil muh fucka."

Someone else aimed a shoe at the boy's ass, but his instincts told him it was coming and he pulled in his cheeks just in time to cushion the blow.

"Foget'chu," Creep shouted the first thing to pop into his mind, but his fight or flight instincts were all flight, no fight. He took off running before somebody decided to beat him up and take his Twinkies. He had an extra mouth to feed, and that was his only plan for dinner.

Pumping his legs as fast as he could without making his Chucks fall apart, the kid turned his radar up to the max, constantly scanning left and right, holding tight to the Twinkies as he made a mad dash back to his building. Over the years, he had gotten good at ducking and dodging the gangs of bullies who always prowled the neighborhood like packs of wild hyenas preying on people for scraps.

The boy sprinted across Division, and then took a shortcut through the Himalaya's parking lot where he weaved his way between cars until finally making a sharp left towards the back-side of the 30 Block. Once he was sure nobody was following him, he changed tracks on the cartoon CD playing in his head to something from Batman, his second favorite soundtrack.

"Dunna-na-na Dunna-na-na…" The fence he left Dead Eye tied to surrounded the playground behind his building. But before he bent the corner, he pulled up a few steps short when he overheard the jumble of voices coming from the other side of the wall. And the voices were awfully familiar, in a bad way, and the words he heard made his heart drop down into his stomach.

"Let's fight it with some pits," a loud, squeaky voice was in the middle of saying, and it was high-pitched like the sound of a teenage boy's before he got the first sprout of pubic hair on his nuts.

"Let's throw it off da roof," a girl offered another suggestion.

"Yeah, see if it lands on its foots," the first squeaky voice seemed to like that idea.

"Dem's cats do dat, not dogs, stupid."

"You stupid."

"Wa-wa-wait." Creep slid out from behind the wall, knowing he was headed into trouble. The situation was way worse than he thought, but he couldn't let them kill his new best friend!

A mob of six juvenile bandits, all bullies the boy had been having a lot of problems with lately, were standing next to the sandbox in a tight circle surrounding a nervous and shaking Dead Eye. Creep didn't really know exactly who they were or where the hell they came from, but their leader was unmistakable and hard to miss, impossible to forget.

To the retard, the head bandit looked just like the ogre from Shrek, with the same big head and fat stomach that stuck out farther than the tips of his shoes and wobbled as he walked. He was on overgrown thirteen-year-old who, if he lived long enough, would always be known as the loud mouth that would never shut the fuck up, and the liar who couldn't tell the truth, even to save his life.

Bandit number two, and the one holding onto Dead Eye's leash, was the leader's right-hand man. She was a bucktoothed nine-year-old with freckles peppering her ugly face. Whenever she opened her mouth, which was too damned often, her voice sounded like fingernails on a chalkboard, or a terrified cat being dragged across a carpet.

Creep didn't let her goofy looks fool him though. He knew she was really the brains of their outfit, and the one making most of the evil suggestions. The last time he crossed paths with the little bandits, he was on his way back from a gas station on Chicago Avenue, where he pumped gas and washed windshields for spare change and loose cigarettes. The gang heard the quarters and dimes jingling in his pockets as he walked, and they corned him over by the Wild End row houses. Instead of wasting time digging through his pockets, they held him down and stole his pants. And it was the evil little girl's idea that had him running five blocks all the way home crying in his tighty whities, in the middle of the day at that.

"Shit, shit, shit..." Creep cursed the bad luck under his breath. A voice in his head screamed a warning to leave Dead Eye to its own luck, and turn around and run, every man for themselves.

The snotty-nosed little boy with the squeaky voice was the first to notice what Creep held in his hands.

"Twinkies!"

In that instant, the gang forgot all about the mutt, and they all bum rushed the boy. Freckle-face got her grimy hands on a pack of the cakes first, and she quickly snatched them out of Creep's surprised fingers. Snot-nose was second. Then they both took off running with the cream-filled goodies, the rest of the crew hot on their heels. The leader, fat and slow, wobbled after them screaming.

"Hey, you muthafuckeeers," his shouts faded as they all disappeared around the side of 630.

Despite what the bullies thought, Creep was only a part-time retard. He had always struggled to hold onto that one good part of his brain. At that moment, it left him with just enough sense to realize he and the dog needed to make their escape while they could. He knew it wouldn't take the gang of juvenile hyenas long to smash those Twinkies and come looking for more.

Creep quickly snatched up Dead Eye's leash, and the mutt followed the boy's lead as if it knew exactly how much their lives were in danger. They ran side by side through the back of the building, around both stairwells, and then to the bank of elevators. There, the boy pressed the call button for the only ride that worked, but the screeching sound of cables and pulleys told him the elevator was somewhere high up above the 12th floor. They didn't have time to wait.

Creep made a snap decision to reroute their getaway back past the front stairwell, the one where crowds of customers waited in long lines to cop fixes. Taking that flight was a no-no, so instead they ducked into the back steps, the ones where the users went to sample their purchases.

The boy and dog dashed past fiends every few steps. They darted around shooters stabbing at their veins in the darkness, crack heads sucking on pipes, and hookers sucking on tricks. By the time they reached the 8th floor landing, they were both winded and out of energy, legs shaking and refusing to take another step.

The retard collapsed on his back. The one-eyed mutt sat back on its dusty tail, tongue dangling from the side of its mouth. None of the bullies knew Creep lived in one of the abandoned apartments, or where it was. So they were both safe for the moment, but just hungry as hell and dead tired.

"Pssst," the sound almost made the boy jump out of his skin. The mutt's ears picked up on the sound, but its one good eye had trouble telling it which way to look.

A black giant, who the retard recognized as Monsta, stood behind them, his size almost filling the entire doorway between the 8th floor landing and the breezeway. The big man motioned for Creep to follow him. The boy wasn't dumb enough to say no, and he certainly didn't have the energy to make another run for it.

A few steps onto the breezeway facing the parking lot, Monsta stopped and looked down at the odd pair of buddies. He took his time shaking a Newport from a pack then lighting it with a match. He blew out a big cloud of smoke that smelled awfully good to the kid.

"Gotta job fo'ya, boy." Monsta reached into his pocket and pulled out a wad of one dollar bills, and then he fanned the stack so Creep could get a good look.

The boy's jaw dropped as he stared wide-eyed at what must have been over a hundred bucks, which was more money than he'd ever seen in his life.

"Wanna get dis munny, boy?" Monsta took another pull on the cigarette then handed it over.

Creep nodded up and down, but he struggled with his words.

"He-he-hell ye-yeah."

To the boy, that much money was like hitting the lottery and cashing out in one lump sum.

"Ands if you duz a gud job, you can make double, maybe even triple."

"Triple?" Creep couldn't believe his luck.

"Yeh, maybe even quadripple."

"Quadripple?" Numbers never were a strong suit for the retard, but even he knew something wasn't right about that math.

"Yeah, Quads, ipples, whuteva," the big flunky peeled off a couple bills for the boy to sample, and then he stuffed the rest back into his pocket.

"Wh-what I gotta d-do?" For Creep, money was about as scarce as a miracle. Even though he was still just a kid, he had lived long enough to know that everything in Cabrini came with strings attached. His eyes followed Monsta's nod out of the chain-link fence and towards the Carter.

"Real simple, real simple..." Of course there were strings attached, and Monsta slowly filled the boy in on the details.

Duke

# Chapter Nine

WahLah got the Goldmine pumping almost overnight, but every dollar going into 714 was a dollar not going into RunThang's building, and the 30 block started feeling the pinch on their profits right away.

At first, the twin wasn't sure who his competition was, or even where his money was leaking to. One call from Angel clued him in though, and he didn't like what he heard. The cop also relayed that same word about their new competition up through his own chain of command, and it didn't take long for one of the bosses back at headquarters to get the team together for a brain-storming session on ways to get their money train back on track.

The usual spot for the crooked crew of cops to meet up was an old abandoned scrapyard right off of I-94 in China Town. The few acres of land on the south side held a small area of Chicago that had been forgotten and left to rot a long time ago. It was the perfect place to pow-wow about their dirty tactics.

"Seems like we pulled the short end of the stick. Run's a fucking fool, and Fool is the real gogetter." Angel was in the middle of expressing his feelings about his partner from the passenger seat of a blacked-out Tahoe idling next to a rusty fence.

"Run isn't just a fool, he's dangerous." The other end of the conversation came from Captain McMassey, who was sitting behind the wheel and chewing on the soggy tip of a fat Cubano. His words were spoken from a long time smoker's throat, and he spit out the twin's name like a bad taste in his mouth,

The captain was an old-time cop with looks that could've popped straight out of an old mobster movie. Gray-streaked red hair gave away his Irish bloodline, and tiny black moles peppered the sun-burned wrinkles crisscrossing his wide and saggy face. He was also a fat slob who wobbled like a walrus when he walked.

The old captain had already heard about the bad blood between the twins, and wars were never productive to the bottom line of a business.

"Run Thang is turning into a liability." McMassey would rather flush their drugs down a toilet than keep propping up the twin's lifestyle.

"Yeah, a liability," Sergeant Alfanzo Basile, the third crook on their crew, yes-manned the conversation from the backseat. He was a short, wiry-framed runt with traditional Italian features, almond complexion, dark eyes, and a long beakish nose that was always red at the tip and sniffling as if frozen on coke. The rest of the cop's face had the kind of look that made mothers walk their kids home from school with 9-1-1 on speed dial. Everyone knew the sergeant as the "Weasel," and he was a typical brown-noser whose opinion didn't really mean shit to the team.

"Before any more of our shit hits the streets, I wanna know what you plan on doin' about those fuckin' twins." The captain kept the conversation between him and Angel. The weasel was just a flunky.

McMassey earned his cop salary by spending his days sitting behind a desk shuffling paperwork and pretending to conduct official police business. His real moneymaker came from coordinating intelligence on drug dealers, from street corners all the way up to connects plugged into pipelines that crossed the border. Once he located their stash spots, a crooked judge signed the search warrants, and then he passed down the necessary info to Angel who then supervised a crew to conduct the raids.

Even bosses have bosses though. McMassey worked for the suits down town, and they had been playing the game of cops and robbers for a very long time. They were all taking too many risks padding their pensions to let a couple project niggas get in the way of their cushy retirements. Plus, the captain had three daughters to put through college, and a wife nagging him to death about it.

"And we already got too many greedy hands eating from the same table." He pounded the dashboard with a meaty fist, mad as hell.

Just last week they gave a low-level runner the shakedown routine, and he flipped like a flapjack on his connects. Three more nights of surveillance uncovered two safe houses, and after the captain got the warrants, Angel kicked in the doors, and the team split a jackpot of twenty-three bricks duck taped and vacuum packed, plus seventy-five racks rubber banded in stacks.

But, just like any business, there were good days and bad days. And whenever times were slow for the north-side crew, there were other S.I.U. units picking up their slack all across the city. Of course they weren't all dirty, or on the same take, and that's where Sgt. Basile earned his stripes. The rat-faced weasel supervised one of the department's evidence storage facilities where all the busts wound up anyway. When the coast was clear, he would quietly switch out the pure coke and heroin coming in for pure garbage. But it was always necessary to leave just enough of the real drugs in each package to test positive in a lab. That way, if the evidence ever came under suspicion, no one could blame him if the streets were pushing that bullshit.

"I think we oughtta get rid of them both." Just like his persona, the captain's mentality was all mobster. "And we don't have time to fuck around about it." To him, the best way to fix a problem was to kill it. Plus, he didn't like his foot soldiers knowing how to think for themselves. Dummies cost a lot less to feed."

"I was thinking we could cut the scrub and sign the all-star," Angel was already thinking one step ahead of his boss.

Their standard operating procedure for dealing with a building or neighborhood they couldn't control was to sit on that spot with a couple squad cars, double-parked and blocking the traffic, while jump out boys faked raids every now and then to scare away the die-hard customers from the inside out. Problem was, pressure like that only lasted for a few days at best, and then there would usually be some kind of retaliation. In this case, those same old tactics wouldn't work in Gangsta City, since the buildings were packed too closely together. No doubt they could shut down the Goldmine and the Carter, but Run Thang wouldn't be able to operate under that pressure either. The cost of war was expensive, even for the police.

"We just gotta put Fool in a situation where he won't have a choice but to get on our team." Whatever the twin's tactics for success were, Angel planned on exposing his playbook, and then making the necessary subs to get his own team back in the game.

"Get him on board, the easy way or the hard way," the fat captain trusted Angel's judgment.

"Yeah, the easy way or the hard way," the Weasel yes-manned in the backseat.

"Because we ain't takin' no more shorts," McMassey didn't have to tell his crew that they were just as replaceable as the twins, either one.

"Yeah, no more shorts." The Weasel had no idea that he was the most replaceable.

"I'll put the pieces in play, but we can't tip our hand." Angel knew it would take a few days to push his plan into motion, and he didn't want Run Thang doing something stupid in the meantime.

Speaking of the devil, the crooked cops spotted the twin's baby-blue Impala pulling through the scrapyard's rusty fence. Run had just gotten his old-school back from a fresh shampoo and rinse, no blow dry, and the ragtop still dripped beads of water as the metallic paint and chrome trim glistened under the moonlight. The big tires crunched gravel as they rolled into a spot between the Tahoe and a matching pair of Crown Vics.

An uneasy quiet greeted the twin when he climbed into the backseat next to the sniffling Weasel, the kind of quiet that said he just cut off a conversation that was all about him. The uneasy atmosphere made Run tense up. He thought the meeting was to scoop a package and lay down some inside info on a new pill factory operating in the suburbs. Angel was always on location for normal drops, sometimes even the sergeant, but Run had only met the captain a few times. The fat bastard hardly ever left the cool A/C of his cushy office downtown, and to see him on the streets meant there had to be trouble brewing,

"WahLah is the one pulling the strings in 714," Angel broke up the twin's thought with his news. "And you know we don't like having our toes stepped on."

"Yeah them's our toes…"

"Shut the fuck up!" The captain's blood pressure had his Irish complexion glowing red-hot. The Weasel's nose twitched, but he kept his lips clamped.

"Then we step our game up," Run Thang gave them his poker-face – blank, no worries.

Competition was nothing new in the projects, and everyone already knew Fool would eventually put a team together and stake a claim to the land that was once his. But Run had no intentions of sharing that information with his partners. Secrets were like aces in the hole, and he never tipped his hand to the cops, crooked or not. They all liked playing with set decks, and while they thought they'd been dealing the only cards in the game, Run had been hedging his bets.

"We don't plan on playing fair." McMassey looked over at Angel to spell out the new plan since, after all, the twin was his partner in Gangsta City.

"I'm going to create some confusion between Fool and his suppliers, and I need you to keep your cool, business as usual, no fuck ups." The detective kept the details of his tactics to himself, but he gave up just enough to keep a leash on Run Thang's jealousy. He had to stall a war for as long as possible.

"Yeah, keep your cool, no fuck ups." The Weasel sniffed and wiped at his nose with the back of a hand.

"If it don't make dollars, it don't make sense." Run kept his poker face on. He didn't have a problem with letting someone else do his dirty work, especially if it was a suicide mission. Besides, he had other plans. He had been holding a grudge against his brother for six years, and he intended to pay that back out of his own pocket – bitch for bitch.

# Chapter Ten

Ever since Fool ran into Sundae at the counter of that McDonald's, he couldn't shake her from his thoughts no matter how hard he tried, and the possibilities of what he could do with her sexy body had him thinking real hard. Problem was, he couldn't make room on his schedule for a Monday lunch, and the next day was no good on her end, so they wound up making arrangements for a mid-week rendezvous at The Float, a new joint in Wrigleyville that served up homemade ice cream and alcohol.

Fool arrived a little early and sat solo sipping on a rum and coke at The Float's main attraction, a long glass bar with a frosty top. As the minutes ticked off the clock, the alcohol mixed with his instincts and made him wonder if he was making a mistake. Was this some kind of new fed tactic, sending a pretty cop to exploit a nigga's weakness? Was Run Thang behind this shit? Of course, cops on the take were nothing new in Chicago, and they were just as greedy as everyone else.

Fool had a lot to think about and not enough time to think about it. He spotted Sundae walking through the door and started to wave for her attention, but he held up when she headed in his direction.

All eyes in the bar followed the sexy detective's walk across the room. She rocked a tiny mini that hung from her hips and seemed to cling to her meaty thighs for dear life. She matched the bright-yellow outfit with a soft cotton top cut off just above her belly button, and the shirt didn't do a damned thing to hold back the pointy tips of her nipples. The color scheme contrasted with her complexion, which could've been honey poured straight out of a beehive.

To Fool, she looked like a sexy piece of fruit, and he wanted to bite the shit out of her. He had to sip back a string of slob before it spilled over his bottom lip.

Despite the medium-sized crowd, Fool managed to save Sundae a seat. But to his surprise, she walked right past as if she didn't even see him. She finally stopped at another empty stool halfway down the bar.

Fool watched from the corner of his eye as she ordered a drink: Grey Goose, Kiwi, and a strawberry mix poured over crushed ice in a glass rimmed with sugar. Almost right away, a small crowd moved in with introductions and flirtatious compliments that she soaked up with a bright smile. Eventually, when her head finally swiveled in his direction, they made eye contact and he gave her a look that said, "What?" But Sundae seemed to look right through him before she spun back around in her stool.

Fool caught on quickly. Sundae liked to play games, and he hoped they were the good kind. He spun around in his seat towards the door, thinking, and he was having the same thoughts he had when they first met. He was definitely thrown off balance and wondering if she designed her moves specifically to get him to pull his guard down. He decided to play along and see where the game went. He just hoped he wasn't playing with fire.

Fool could see by the look on her face that the small talk was quickly turning stale. As he got closer to the bottom of his glass, he felt footsteps behind him.

"Excuse me," Sundae's reflection was gorgeous in the mirror across from the bar. "Do I know you from somewhere?" she spoke softly, but loud enough to be heard over the conversations going on around them.

"Maybe." Fool turned halfway around with his glass paused almost at his lips. Sundae was even prettier than he remembered.

"Aren't you that actor who played in *Menace II Society*?" A sweet smile had her eyes lit up.

"Uh-uh," Fool shook his head.

"Oh yeah, you're a rapper, right?" She acted as though she struggled for a name.

"Nope, not me." Fool was game to play along.

"Sounds like there's an interesting story behind that," she reached out a hand and Fool took it. "Name's Sundae. Can I get you another drink?" She slid in next to him without waiting for a reply.

"I don't mind, but I'm waiting for someone," Fool sat his glass on the bar's frosty top.

"Girlfriend?"

He shook his head. "Just met her. She's a cop, and a sexy one." He said just enough to keep the lead on her.

Besides, Fool found himself enjoying watching her talk. Her lips were painted a luscious shade of cherry-red, and her tongue reminded him of a moist strawberry. Even her breath smelled like something that could quench his thirst, passion fruit and mango, delicious.

"What a coincidence," Sundae could almost see his thoughts, and she fed his imagination some more eye-candy with a playful swipe of her tongue along the sticky sugar rimming her glass. She made it twist and turn up and over the edge before taking a cool dip in the icy drink.

Fool followed the slow, seductive movements as her tongue slid up the little straw and hugged the tiny hole at the top. The acrobatics almost made him rise up and give her performance a standing ovation. He wanted to ask for an encore, but instead, he down-shifted his excitement to a lower gear so he could keep a grip on his composure.

"I'm waiting on someone, too." Sundae finally finished her original thought.

"Oh yeah?" Fool spotted a cute couple vacating a table in a quiet corner. He made a suggestion. "While we wait on our dates, how about we get to know each other over a few bites of chocolate?"

"My sweet tooth could use a treat," she let him lead her across the room by a hand, and as they sat down, a table girl was already walking up with a menu.

Fool ordered for them both, but instead of two separate bowls, he figured it would be more fun to share one. He went for a tasty desert called the "Chocolate Conundrum." It was a frosty concoction of every kind of chocolate ever invented, all topped with chips, swirls, shaving, syrup, and whipped cream. When the serving girl spun off, the twin switched his focus over to small talk.

"Is you name spelled A-Y or A-E?" Of course he already knew, but he had a feeling that he was going to like the way she said it.

"Just like the ice cream."

"I'm feeling that." Fool was right.

"Sounds tasty?"

"Yummy." Fool reached across the table, and for a second, their eyes locked when their hands touched. Then he gave her a look that told her how bad he wanted a taste.

Sundae picked up on the vibe and passed it right back with a look of her own that silently said, "I might melt in your mouth."

"So." Fool leaned forward, the other conversations buzzing around the ice cream shop forced him to turn up the volume on his conversation. "Do you like being the center of attention?"

"What do you mean?" Sundae met him halfway across the table.

"Can't you tell when all eyes are on you?" Fool waved his hand around the room at the men and women who seemed as if they couldn't stop staring at the sexy stranger. "Even the table girl was sizing you up."

Sundae gave him a knowing smile without bothering to look around. Of course she knew exactly how good she looked. Men had been rubber necking her curves ever since she was thirteen.

"That one over there looks like he's star-struck." Fool nodded over at a tall white dude, jock-type, sitting across a table from his own date. His eyes kept swinging back in Sundae's direction like a compass needle pointing north, and he was paying no attention to his girl or whatever she was jabbering on about.

"What do you think he's thinking?" Sundae added a new play to the game.

"Hmm," Fool thought about it for a second. "He's guessing you're a college student and aspiring actress."

"Uh-uh," Sundae frowned playfully. "That's too weak, I can do better than that." She pointed out a tall blond sporting varsity sweats, Northwestern University volleyball. The woman was using the bar's mirror to mask her stares. Sundae read her mind. "She's thinking I'm one discovery away from being a super-model."

That got Fool laughing again, and he knew he had to step up his game on the next one. He spotted a group of nerd-types sitting around a table with no dates. None of them bothered being shy about their necks craning, and it seemed as though they were even placing bets on what she did for a living.

"One side is thinking stripper, while the other two are hoping you're a porn star, and they're all picturing you naked."

That tickled Sundae's funny bone and she almost fell out of her seat. After she regained her composure, Fool added, "And so am I."

The table girl arrived with their orders before Fool could get a response. He used the break in their conversation to switch gears in case he was moving too fast.

"So, what makes a sexy cop go bar-hopping in the middle of the week?"

Sundae waited for the girl to set the bowl down with a couple spoons and walk away. Then she leaned over the table and whispered loudly, "I'm undercover, looking for bad guys."

Fool grabbed a spoon and dug into the bowl for a taste-test. Then he leaned forward like he had his own scandalous secret to tell.

"I'm a bad guy. Reeaal bad."

"I already know," Sundae said to his surprise, and then she burst his bubble even more. "I know about your brother and his crooked partner, too."

Fool slammed on the brakes, 60 down to 0 in one second flat. Again, he struggled to keep his cool, but he couldn't keep his eyes from darkening with suspicion. So was he right all along? Was this a shakedown, or even a trap? His muscles tensed, preparing for the worst.

Sundae sensed the sudden change in their playful atmosphere. And she quickly elaborated before he threw up his guard and spoiled the fun.

"I'm S.I.U. just like Angel, but we aren't on the same team, and we damn sure aren't friends." In other words, her badge was just as dirty as his. Of course Fool was no fool. He knew the benefits of teaming up with a cop, but he never felt the need for their services, and they never felt the need for his.

"Why me?" He got straight to the point, no more beating around the bush.

"I work out of the west side, Harrison and Kedzie," Sundae talked fast. Fool didn't open the door for her all the way, but it was cracked, and she got her toe in before he slammed it shut. "But opportunity is shrinking and competition is tight. So, I'm looking to spread my wings, maybe even take on a partner of my own."

Fool let that marinate on his mind, but only for a second, while she swirled her spoon around the frosty bowl of ice cream.

"What can you do for me that I can't do for myself?"

"Bribes, busts, and traffic stops put more bricks in my hands than the best connects in the city." Sundae kept her response short and simple, but then she added one more very important piece. "Plus, sooner or later, Angel is going to come knocking on your door, and he'll have a nasty crew with him. If you plan on lasting long, you're going to need back up."

Fool contemplated the possibilities. He already had a solid connect with a team of go-getters, and everyone was getting fat with no complaints. But at the same time, he knew those profits would draw attention, and Angel would come knocking sooner rather than later. Also, Run Thang definitely had the upper hand with a cop on his side. Either way, Fool wasn't ready to commit, at least not without investigating the ups and downs from every angle.

"So, this date was part of the act, just business?" Disappointment hung over his shoulders like a dark cloud, and he felt it like a dead weight.

"First impressions mean everything." Sundae paused with a look that reminded him that he wasn't the only one who was game conscious. "Besides, I'm single, looking, and I like what I see."

Her words helped lift Fool's spirits and pull his guard back down, from super-max with gun towers and barbed-wire to minimum security, no fence. Sundae started playing with the dessert, and she dipped her tongue into the chocolate on her spoon, just for his viewing pleasure. Once the corners of his mouth started twitching, as if he wanted to smile from his own thoughts, she asked, "So what are you thinking?"

Fool hesitated only for a second. "You look like you taste way better than this ice cream." His imagination was already undressing her, like pealing the wrapper off a juicy lollipop.

That got the smile returning to both of their faces. The game was back on and Sundae took it to another level. "You wanna lick me?"

Duke

# Chapter Eleven

"Mmm," Sundae was showing off her vocal skills. "Ooooh…"
"Aaah," Fool blew on the hook.
"Squeak, squeak, squeak…" Bedsprings produced the beat.

They got back to Fool's Bucktown apartment as fast as traffic would let them, and inside, they didn't waste a second getting their clothes snatched off and tossed, sheets tangled and twisted. Sundae kept the fun and games non-stop all the way from the bar, and her imagination was as wild as a nymphomaniac twerking on X in a porno flick.

Erotic fantasy, episode-1: Sundae was on top, straddling Fool's face like the back of a Ducati 916, fire-engine red, and his tongue was the leather seat. The powerful engine was the growl in his throat, and he had the needle on Sundae's tach sweeping past 9k, 10k, then wide open throttle-no rev-limit- and her body was loving every wonderful vibration.

The vivid scenes of her fantasy sent them zooming down a long straightaway at full speed. The black asphalt rushed by under fat rubber tires until they inclined up a shallow hill. Her thighs tightened their grip, and just as the frontend crested the top, she threw the bike into a quick left. Her flexing muscles began to let up for a brief second deep into the corner, but a shake of Fool's head between her thighs tossed her into a hard right, and she hung on for dear life.

The Ducati blasted out of the final turn of Sundae's mental racetrack like a rocket. Her body was exhausted from what could've been a hundred laps nonstop, but instead of crossing the finish line, she grabbed the side of Fool's head to ease up on the throttle. They pulled over to the side of the road where she breathlessly informed him of the warning light flashing and glowing red-hot on her dash. Sundae's little motor was overheating, so Fool brought her revs down slowly, 3k, 2k, until he had her purring at a smooth idle.

The sexy detective wasn't the only one writing the script to this fantasy. The twin penciled in his own part. He wanted to be inside of her so they could finish the race together. He was fiending to feel her powerful contractions pulling and squeezing, especially the tremble of her thighs around his waist as she lost control. Fool slid up to make that happen, and for a moment, he could even feel his own legs shaking from an anxiousness to dive into her.

"Wait, wait," Sundae stopped him with her hands and then rolled over for a better position on the starting line, on her hands and knees. No doubt, she liked to fuck, and more than most, but she always kept it squeaky. She nodded over at a pile of rubbers they'd scattered across the bed earlier.

Fool made a quick search for one that glowed in the dark. Blue was his favorite, and while he fumbled to slide it on, Sundae helped get his blood pumping for maximum hardness and a tighter fit. Pink-painted fingernails gently caressed the toned curves of her inner thighs as she spread her legs and arched her back so he could get a good look at what was waiting for him.

Sundae's pussy stuck out like a target, and Fool was a sniper with more aim than a sharpshooter. But he struggled with the condom. It was too tight and he was straining not to explode and blow it up like a balloon.

Sundae used the pause to catch her breath and let the temp on her hot little engine cool down a bit. She could still feel the tickling tips of a tingle crawling up her spine, and if Fool got his dick anywhere near her, she'd blow a gasket and leave him crossing that finish line by himself. Plus, the timeout gave her imagination a chance to turn the page to the next episode of her wild fantasy, but she could still use his help with a tease.

"Tell me how bad you want this pussy," she said looking back over her shoulder, pretty eyes blinking bashfully.

"Like a clucka wants crack." The strength of Fool's erection told Sundae all she needed to know, but that still wasn't good enough for her.

"Uh-uh," she shook her head. She wanted him fiending for it harder than a junkie for a needle. "I wanna know how baaad you wanna fuck this pussy."

Sundae nibbled on her bottom lip while she stroked her shaved kitty from behind. In case he didn't already know how wet she was inside, she spread it open and showed him.

Fool's mind stuttered for words. That kind of pink was another one of his favorite colors, and it always got his heart racing whenever he saw it. At the moment, his pulse pumped so hard it made his dick twerk to an invisible beat. Sundae watched as it stretched and stretched and stretched, until it looked as if he was about to tear a ligament or dislocate a bone. When he finally found his voice, he let her know exactly what he was thinking.

"I wanna beat that pussy like it stole something."

"Oooh," Sundae liked that idea. "Like a gorilla?"

"Silverback."

Sundae's imagination went flying off on another wild trip, and she was thinking exotic jungle, maybe somewhere in the Congo.

Erotic fantasy, episode 2:  She was a young innocent princess strolling along a winding riverbank when, all of a sudden, she spotted a big black warrior stalking her from some nearby bushes, too close for her to run.

Sundae's hand unconsciously released its playful grip on her inner thigh, and then she tangled her fingers into the pillow in front of her. The little African princess dug her knees into the mattress and braced herself to be conquered. "Come take this pussy."

Fool reacted in a split second, poking and stabbing, hammering and pounding. Every time his hips rolled with the soft curves of her ass, he paused with a deep grind that sparked enough friction to get them both lost inside of the fantasy. And to his surprise, Sundae met every blow with a counter punch of her own, and she bucked it harder than a bronco.

Sundae felt her body rising from the mattress, being flipped and flopped, and turned in different positions. She blinked rapidly through a blurry vision that had her wondering if she really was somewhere in a deep jungle being raped by a warrior. Fool's weapon penetrated her from every angle, over and over, and he had the stamina of a champion.

Fool read her body language like he was bilingual, and he didn't miss any of her indicators either, the flushed look on her gorgeous face, or the bright sparkle lighting up her almond shaped eyes. He watched as her focus shifted from him to somewhere far, far away, and then back to him again. When Sundae's bucking finally climaxed into a shudder that quaked all the way from her spine to her knees, Fool paused his pounding in time to soak in the vibrations and intense heat building up inside her. The look of her losing control beneath him was the spark that finally made him detonate.

Blast after blast gripped and pulled him in deeper and deeper until he released everything he had to give her. Fool's shaky arms finally collapsed, and at the same time, Sundae's energy drained until she was just as weak. She loosened the tension of her thighs around his hips, and they spent the last few minutes of consciousness wrapped in each other's arms. Both of their imaginations were completely spent, along with their bodies, no speedy recovery, no Mandingo all night, and no more ideas for erotic fantasy, episode 3.

# Chapter Twelve

Sundae lounged against a soft pile of harem pillows, stripped naked and topped-off like the real thing, whipped cream and strawberries, while Fool sipped shots of X.O. out of her bellybutton.

"You taste like a cognac float."

"You're a kinky crook." Sundae enjoyed being his dessert, but she wanted to fuck some more, so she offered him an extra serving, no change. "Banana split?"

Fool reluctantly declined her offer. He shot off the last bullet in his gun almost two hours ago, and his legs were still shaky, back still weak. His body couldn't have felt more drained if he had just got done knocking out a ninety minute Insanity DVD, playing a pick-up game on the courts, and then running a 10k marathon.

Sundae had just got done filling him in on her fantasies, and their African Safari. "You fucked me so hard I was confused for a minute." She kept him laughing while stroking his ego at the same time.

"You must'a ran into King Kong in that jungle." Fool was smiling so hard his cheeks were sore. He slid off the edge of the bed to hunt down his jeans, and then he dug through a pocket for a Newport.

Sundae stretched out with her hands behind her head, body still sticky from the whipped cream, while she lazily watched Fool's cuts ripple through his muscles as he searched the room for a lighter.

"Got any ideas for a sequel?" she asked as he grabbed an ashtray and climbed into a cozy spot next to her.

"I don't usually fantasize, too busy concentrating."

"Hmm," she sort of liked that answer, as long as he was concentrating on her. "I was thinking somewhere with a white sandy beach, maybe an island. Wanna go to the Bahamas?"

"Are we a couple, or strangers? Any special guest?" Fool smiled at the possibilities.

"There's a few women, sexy, bikinis," Sundae arched an eyebrow with a sly smile that rewarded him for his creative input. That gave Fool one more reason to find the sassy detective irresistible, and the deeper their conversations got, the more he found to like. But, still he had to constantly remind himself that the naked girl next to him was the police. He was new to those kinds of games, but not the players, and he had always considered the law as his enemy by birth. So, he decided to save any thoughts of a possible ménage a tois for later.

"We need to talk about real life, and what's next." It was time to get serious.

Sundae definitely wanted to drag out the fun for as long as possible, pleasure before business, but forming their kind of partnership wasn't as easy as shaking hands. And it would be best if they ironed out the details sooner rather than later.

Partners in crime, fuck-buddies, or a relationship with a foundation, they all sounded like good ideas to Sundae, but first she decided to give Fool a quick rundown of her own criminal history so he could see for himself where she came from and where she was trying to go.

"Vice squad…" That was Sundae's beat until about nine months ago when the department upgraded her badge to special investigation unit, S.I.U. Recently, she'd mostly worked what was left of the west side projects, which wasn't much.

"Rockwell Gardens?" Fool guessed right, and she nodded her head. The city had been putting the dynamite and bulldozers to those buildings just like all the other high rise projects around Chicago.

"Promotions meant possibilities…" she continued. Like every cop operating with S.I.U., Sundae signed up for the opportunity of making big bucks, and just like Angel, she had no intentions of fighting crime. When she was first transferred, she was teamed up with a veteran partner named Mike who was closing in on his retirement in a few months, at the ripe old age of thirty-five. The streets had been very generous to his bank account, and he was kind enough to show her the ropes and pass on a few contacts who were always willing to donate to a good cause. And, at the time, every dope-boy in the hood lined up to get the sexy detective in their pockets. Those idiots actually believed having a cop on their payroll made them instant big timers, Scarface or Pueblo Escobar, and they all made a claim for the kingpin's throne.

"Ha," Fool couldn't help but laugh at suckers like that. So, what' up wit the change of scenery? Cabrini ain't the Westside." He knew a few of the gangstas in the Rockwells, and they held down a couple of those buildings like high-rise fortresses.

"Don't I know it," Sundae rolled her eyes. "At one time, I had three buildings checking-in a couple grand apiece every week, all for worthless promises and bogus information. Only problem was, those stupid motherfuckers thought gang banging was more important than making money, and they wouldn't stop shooting at each other."

At the moment, the city had their bulldozers posted, waiting to tear down the last of the Rockwell high-rises. Meanwhile, the Feds were preparing for the fallout of thousands of project niggas scattered into the nearby neighborhoods, and times were too risky for a crooked cop to get caught up in that mix.

"Yeah." Fool heard about those niggas warring over bullshit. But there were twenty-something buildings in Cabrini. "What made me stick out of the crowd?"

"I did my homework." Sundae gave it to him straight. Every street corner and project building in Chicago had someone claiming it, and depending on the gang in the particular area, there were usually one or two people holding the deed on the land. When Sundae first went digging through the records on Cabrini, Run Thang's name was on most of the titles. She was already clued in on the reputation of the local S.I.U. operating in the district, and she knew they wouldn't appreciate any visitors. But just like any greedy landlord, hollering in the right ear and lining the right pockets would get the doors open. In the case of S.I.U., stepping on the wrong toes would start a war.

So, Sundae dug a little deeper into the details, and eventually she recognized an opportunity. With Run Thang, his jealousy fed his hate, his hate made mistakes, and she knew it was just a matter of time before he got the crown knocked off his head. Plus, Fool's recent release was front page news in Gangsta City, and he was the obvious heir to the throne.

"I can dig your tactics, no doubt. But like you said earlier, promises, promises. I don't need'em, and running a few stacks every week to somebody I'm fucking sounds like trickin' off to me." Fool could understand a cop's side of the bargain. For them, it was only good business. But a crook might as well wipe his ass with that money, and then flush it down the toilet.

"Think about this," Sundae came prepared with her sales pitch, and her product didn't need a thirty-day money-back guarantee. "Besides the feds, S.I.U makes the biggest drug seizures in the city, and we flip more informants than IHOP flips pancakes. When my connects move bricks, they move them in eighteen wheelers." She let him soak up that information and marinate on it for a minute.

"I got my own plugs." Fool didn't really need a matchmaker, since that was already his own MO, but he did need some more players on his team if he expected to compete with his brother. "So, what up wit Run Thang's partner, Angel?"

Sundae smiled that knowing smile. She started out with the inside scoop on McMassey, his shakedown tactics, and how the Weasel pulled a weekly switcheroo at the evidence warehouse. After she filled Fool in on the captain's resume, she started on Angel's, and that information came with a warning.

"He's a real dirty son of a bitch. If they think you're putting a squeeze on their profits, he won't hesitate to make it real tight on you. Something like an eight by ten cell down state, or a shallow grave somewhere in the boondocks.

Fool didn't doubt it, and he would most definitely take heed to her warning. Niggas didn't become successful in the game without making smart decisions, and nobody grew old in the streets without knowing how to watch their backs, especially in the projects where life's expiration date was barely thirty-five years.

"So, what's the deal? How do you feel about playing tag-team with a cop?" Sundae kept it a hundred, and then threw the ball back in Fool's court.

To the twin, it seemed like the sexy detective was a mind reader. But he could see the future as well, and he was already looking way past the projects.

"To tell you the truth, I let my light-weight handle the day-to-day grind. I'm focused on bigger and better things." Fool ran down the business model to his new beautiful partner, one without the violence and day-to-day risks Run Thang and his crew kept themselves mixed up in.

Fool had a direct line to every Gangsta hood in the city, from all sides and way out to the suburbs. Plus, he could even cross a few state lines and be welcomed with open arms. But he knew Sundae's people patrolled more routes than UPS and FedEx put together, with inside info to keep them safe. And, if they combined their talents, they could build a pipeline that would flood the streets like hurricane Katrina. Besides renting floors in Cabrini and collecting property taxes, Knuck could help them play matchmaker between the heavies at the top of the game, who were anxious to drop their loads, and the light-weights on the bottom, who were thirsty for a plug. They could chop the profits down the middle, no need to be greedy, and if everything went according to plan, they could all retire early.

Duke

# Chapter Thirteen

For heroin addicts, the early bird catches the worm, and in Gangsta City, 7:00am was when most of those pigeons clucked. It was the height of rush-hour traffic, when all of the buildings swarmed with fiends gassing up their tanks for a hard day's work. The one's punching clocks needed to get their fix in order to function for a full nine to five without breaking down. The unemployed just wanted to get high before they hit the streets and hustled.

Rush-hour was also an easy time to catch the dope-boys slipping, and a perfect time for Angel and S.I.U. to conduct a raid. The big detective called the early morning plays from a tinted-out Explorer parked on a demolition site on Division, about a block down and across the street from 714. An old shoe factory in the process of being bulldozed was his cover, and he blended in with a few other unmarked vehicles pretending to be a part of the demolition company.

Angel leaned low in the Ford, watching through the lens of a spotter scope as traffic moved in and out of the Goldmine. He kept the windows cracked to listen in on the distant shouts of sales pitches competing for every dollar being spent.

"Bottom of the 9th!"

"Knockout blows!"

"Dope so good it'll make you suck yo own dick!"

Users were easy to pick out from the non-users. Fiends on their way in to shop walked towards the buildings with sluggish steps, noses runny and eyes crusty. The shoppers who had already copped rushed away from the high-rises with an extra pep in their steps, anxious to get home and unwrap their purchases. They all kept their eyes peeled for the jump-out boys who were ready to lay niggas down, and the local scavengers sizing up the road kill.

The workers inside were moving at the same frantic pace. Somewhere on the third, fourth, and fifth floors, pack-men rung up customers at the cash registers, fingers fumbling in the darkness with small knotted sandwich bags while their partners counted money. Runners stood by ready to make trips back and forth from the safe house and keep the shelves fully stocked with merchandise. The detective adjusted the focus on his scope and zoomed in on a woman dressed in dirty rags and standing like a zombie next to the front entrance. She was asleep on her feet, chin planted in her chest with a long string of slob drooling from the corner of her cracked lips. Every few seconds, the nod made her knees buckle until she caught herself and straightened back up. The dance made her look like she was bobbing to a beat only she could hear.

A customer walked up and said something that brought her back to life. She lifted her head for a brief second, and Angel laughed when he recognized her face. Vicky was her name, and even though she was young, about twenty-one, she was sort of a project celebrity. A little over a year back, Vicky broke a city record when she got busted for shoplifting over a hundred times in less than six months.

Once upon a time, Vicky would've been called cute. That was before her ex-pimp worked her through rain, sleet, and snow, and then beat her ass like a runaway slave. Eventually, hepatitis popped up, stole her glamour, and left her looking gruesome.

Angel knew that the girl's present employer was the crew operating out of the Goldmine, and she was supposed to be directing traffic through the front entrance. Evidently, Fool and WhaLah allowed their employees to sleep on the job. Run Thang would've had her tossed down a flight of steps, if he was in a good mood. A bad mood would've gotten her booked for a flight off the roof.

The detective fired up the Explorer then grabbed his Motorola and gave two chirps. "Team in position," came back over the speaker, and he "10-4'd" the call then gave the go ahead to move in. He bent a wide U-turn through traffic on Division, and behind him, two Crown Vics and a Chevy followed his lead. Ten more blue and white squad cars rolled in hot from the other side of 714 with their lights, sirens, and full battle gear making as much nose as possible. They surrounded the building on all sides, no one in, no one out.

The deal was to let the crews inside know what was coming, no surprises. Running into one of Cabrini's building unannounced was a sure-fire way to get shot. Besides, Angel knew damn well it was next to impossible to catch anyone inside with so much as a crumb.

By the time the taskforce could rush the front and back, the crews would have already scattered throughout the apartments, their money and drugs stashed in a hundred different hiding spots where nothing could be pinned on anybody. Most of the gangs dumped their dirt down the apartment heating vents that were straight-shots to the basement. When the coast was clear, they'd pop a few screws and get whatever got missed in the raid. Whatever the police popped would get chalked up as a loss.

It was the oldest trick in the book. All the S.I.U. vets knew it, and all the mobs in the projects knew they knew. Cat and Mouse was the name of their never-ending game, but who was the cat and who was the mouse wasn't always easy to tell. The crews were always changing the plays and rotating their routines, and the cops were constantly adapting with new tactics to bust them up. They figured out ways to infiltrate the mobs and knock off their heads, then the mobs grew new ones, and either side wouldn't hesitate to pick each other off the first chance they got.

That time, Angel had a move no one had seen played yet, and he broke up his play into two separate stunts. The first was just a fake, the second a knockout punch and it all began with his S.I.U. team finally inside the building. Once they made sure all the stairwells and breezeways were deserted with no stragglers, the detectives went about their routines conducting searches door to door, top to bottom, hitting all the obvious spots and pretty much spending about a half-hour bullshitting.

The captain gave Angel a key to 1606, a vacant apartment all the way on the top floor. After he was sure none of the nosy neighbors were paying attention, he peeled off nine of his own handpicked crew and they all ducked inside. That part of the plan was for them to sit tight while the rest of the taskforce turned up the volume on their noise to let everyone in the building know that they were leaving, raid over.

So far so good, except for the part about the apartment being empty. Angel spotted the first indicator that something wasn't quite right when he went to unlock the front door that wasn't locked like it was supposed to be. Then, when the ten detectives walked inside, a god-awful wave of funk blasted them in the face, something like ass and armpits mixed with a lot of stale piss.

Everyone tried to avoid the smell by breathing through their mouths as they piled into the tiny one-bedroom apartment, but that only made them taste the stink. Next, they tried taking small sips of air until their noses adjusted.

The second problem no one planned for was the wall to wall piles of garbage crammed into the front room. Thousands of roaches scattered in every direction as mice the size of rats crunched on the bugs like M&M's. And the trash wasn't even the worst of the decoration. Most of the bricks had been knocked out of the walls to get at the copper wires and pipes. The toilet in the bathroom overflowed with mushy turds, and no one could close the door to block off the smell because somebody stole it off the hinges a long time ago.

Their final surprise popped up when the old dope fiend Ghost stumbled out of the bedroom mumbling, "What da fuh?" He had one arm tied off with a shoestring, and it oozed blood from several spots where the needle missed his veins. His yellow eyes bugged out wide with just as much surprise as he got a load of the cops around him.

"Muh fucka, ya'll gotta warrant?" Blood splattered out of his rotten mouth as he talked, and it sent all of the detectives jumping back a few steps.

Angel recognized the old bum, and before one of his fatal diseases could get anywhere near him, he pulled out a Taser and painted Ghost with an infrared dot.

"Get your nasty ass back in that room, and don't say shit until we get out of here."

There was no way Angel could let the bum walk out of the apartment. Ghost wouldn't hesitate to hit the alarm button in the projects and let everyone know what the police were up to. The only way the second stage of the detectives' plan could go off without a hitch was if absolutely no one saw it coming.

After Angel forced the fiend back into the room, the crew went around opening all the small windows in the apartment, and then they stood around trying not to touch anything while they waited for the signal to initiate stage 2.

Duke

# Chapter Fourteen

Fool had a few early morning orders that needed filling across town. Since his bottom-line couldn't afford any more losses like the one from the other day, he had to personally supervise the runners while they made the drops. After seeing to that business, he swung through the south-side to scoop Tameeka and Mini-me from her mom's crib, and then they all headed back north, baby girl pushing the whip, Fool kicked-back on the passenger side scrolling through messages on his Facebook, and mini-me in the backseat slinging pickles from a cheese burger.

Besides a few other orders and a couple friend requests that Fool shot down, everything on his schedule was up to date. He was supposed to meet up with Sundae so she could upgrade his tactics with some inside info on S.I.U. and how they operated, but they hadn't set a time for that date yet. The twin knew he shouldn't be procrastinating on something so important, since the crooked cops had a lot of dirty tricks up their sleeves, and Angel's were the filthiest.

On that same note, Tameeka had been sweating over that heat she knew would eventually come, and she didn't want to lose another man to the penitentiary. At that very moment, she was in the middle of sharing her thoughts about quitting the game.

"…constantly ducking cops and grimy niggas is too hectic to be healthy. And when you pause your life to do a bid, you gotta start all over from scratch when you get back out. Plus, the streets got expiration dates on 'em, and you gotta plan your own retirement cuz the game don't offer 401k's."

Fool appreciated her concern, no doubt, and he soaked up the advice like a sponge.

"Best believe, hustling on the streets gotta be way harder than running a real business. But there's light at the end of the tunnel..." He had already let her in on some of his goals for the future.

Just like he perfected the art of gorilla marketing, and the techniques of using flunkies on the frontlines, he knew he could apply those same cut throat tactics to a legit enterprise. But of course that was easier said than done. Plus, he didn't have to remind Tameeka that he never did anything legal in his life. So, staying true to his MO, instead of jumping into a new game head-first, he wanted to get his feet wet first by bankrolling people who were already on that side of life and knew what they are doing. And, even when he decided to take that leap, he'd have to be just as careful, because the only thing the police hated more than a drug dealer was a drug dealer going legit.

Fool's phone "Cha-chinged" in his lap and a pair of boxing gloves popped up on the screen.

"What's up?"

"The mine got hit." Knuck had bad news, which wasn't really new or all that bad. Every building in the projects got their turn for the police's attention, and they were used to being raided at least once a week.

"What's the damage?"

"A few cuts and scrapes, but we'll be back on our feet in a few minutes. But keep your head up coming thru." Knuck made sure cuz wasn't riding dirty.

"Bending the corner now." Fool hung up, and then he gave Tameeka directions. "The dick eaters knocked one of the buildings. Circle the lot before you pull up."

In the projects, all it took was a quick glance to see if the police were on location. Hustlers were quick to clear the fire lane, cluckas and fiends faded into the background, and the lookouts no longer looked out. Gangsta City would turn into a ghost town, but at the moment, the buildings buzzed like beehives, which meant the coast was clear. Tameeka pulled the Caddy into a slot on the back side of the Goldmine.

"Rocks. Blows. Weed, Pills," shouts were loud, and drug traffic was thick.

Tameeka spotted Creep hanging around the green dumpster behind the Carter. It looked as if he was smoking on something rolled up, probably cigarette butts, and he was holding a mangy mutt by a rusty collar.

"I feel sorry for that poor dog," she shook her head with a sad face.

"That's Creep," Fool barely knew the boy. The last time he saw the retard, a gang of bullies were chasing him through the lot, and they were hot on his heels.

"Creep," Tameeka repeated the name with a sour look and a shiver. Something about the kid's demeanor gave her a vibe that was all bad. "I don't like that boy."

"I gotta holla at Knuck about some business. I'll meet you upstairs in a few." Fool leaned across the seat and stuck his tongue down her throat. Then he started unstrapping Mini-me from the back.

"And get these pickles off my seats." Fool remembered something he wanted to ask Tameeka. "You like women?"

"Nigga, what?" Her jaw dropped.

Jealousy was obviously no issue between them, and Fool had no hesitations with driving recklessly on the subject, but he definitely caught Tameeka off guard with his question. Even so, she was surprised it took him so long to ask.

"At least you didn't say no." Fool spun off before she did say no.

Knuck stood by the back entrance of the Goldmine with WahLah and a couple youngsters from the crew, Lil Rob and Big'em. They were turning up a 40 of Old E with a couple blunts in rotation.

"What up, Gangsta?" Fool flashed a pitchfork, and they all responded with hand grenades, sign language for G's up.

"Struggle," everyone seemed to say at the same time. Big'em offered Fool the end of a blunt, but the twin shook it off. It was too early to get stuck on stupid.

"What's good in da hood?" Fool slid his phone into a pocket then leaned against a railing.

"Same shit, different day. Police tryna get greasy at rush-hour." Knuck dismissed the raid as just another stunt to fuck with their money, no big deal.

"Fuck'em," Fool started to shift the conversation towards other business when he realized he spoke a little too soon.

"Blue and whites northbound on Larrabee," warning shouts went up from the lookouts all over the parking lot. Then they were quickly followed at the front of the building.

"Crown Vic. Three times on Division," someone on the roof hollered down. Tweakers heading inside busted U-turns and scattered like roaches. Peddlers packed up their merchandise and walked off. The buzz of Gangsta City came to a sudden stop as the brakes got slammed on everyone's hustles.

"Handle that," WahLah gave Lil Rob and Big'em instructions as they dipped into the back of 714. Of course, the crew already knew the drill.

Squads and unmarked cars of all kinds and colors hit the lot from every angle. Chargers, Crown Vics, and Impala's all pointed their blacked-out grills toward the cousins. Fool didn't believe in coincidences, and he had a sneaky feeling the police were on some hi-tech bullshit. The only times they ever doubled-back so quickly were when they were trying to be slick with new tricks.

Him and Knuck ducked through the back door while they still had a chance to make a getaway. The twin climbed the first set of steps on the left while Knuck cut through the lobby and took the second set. Fool wasn't really worried though, since he wasn't dirty, but running from the police was still second nature. And besides, the police had never been known to play by the book, unless they were trying to hit you in the head with it.

Fool quickly made the third floor landing, then through the stairwell exit and across the lobby to the elevators. There, he jabbed at the call button and listened for a quick second. The elevator was right above him so he waited, but not for long. Before the doors slid halfway open, he could see that the inside was clogged with dark-blue bullet-proof vests and gold badges.

The twin's instincts spun him around and told him to make another dash up the steps, but the "Click-clack" of heavy metal behind his head told him something different. A swarm of infrared dots danced across the front of his shirt and held his feet glued to the spot.

"Mr. Barksdale," Fool had never heard the voice before, but he didn't need an introduction to know who it belonged to. He turned around with his hands up, and S.I.U. surrounded him from all sides, no more running.

Duke

# Chapter Fifteen

The raid turned out to be just another fake stunt by S.I.U. At first, Fool thought he recognized the move from one of their old playbooks, one he called "Inny-minny-miney-moe."

Whenever there was an unsolved crime in Cabrini, whoever's name popped up in a hat got matched up with that case, and sometimes it was a body. But the current shakedown routine seemed to be new, and even though Fool had never been one of its victims, Sundae boot-legged a copy of Angel's game plan, so he had the move figured out the minute he was cuffed and tossed into the back of the detective's blacked-out Explorer. The raid was an intimidation tactic, meant to warn the Goldmine's crew while their boss got taken for a spin around the block.

The crooked detective rode shotgun while a ratty-looking Italian with sergeant stripes did the driving.

"I don't give a fuck about a bullshit beef between brothers. This is about money." According to Angel, Fool could either work for them, or pack his shit and move to another town.

"And we ain't askin', we's tellin'." The Weasel took his turn laying down their scare tactics.

But, to their disappointment, Fool shook off the threats like water rolling off a ducks back. At the same time, he kept his poker-face in place. The object of the game was to keep his cool and never let them see him sweat.

"Deal sounds sweet, but I'm tryna watch my figure," He knew any sign of a crack in his armor, and they would be at him like a pack of pit bulls on a puppy. "Besides, I'm a solo act, so you can keep the deals for yo suckas, and the threats for yo chumps."

Fool was also wondering if Run had a part in this stunt, or was his team out scouting for new talent and ready to retire his number. Either way, Fool wrote himself a mental note to make sure his own squad learned from this experience. From then on, all police would be counted coming in and going out of the buildings, with full sweeps of the vacant apartments before shop reopened.

Angel was letting his anger show. Blood pounded at his temples and boiled behind the whites of his eyes. The big detective could see that Fool recognized their act as just a façade, but the twin's speculation was only half-right. True, Angel wanted him on their team, but McMassey wanted him dead. Thankfully, the cop had more than one trick up his sleeve to get Fool to accept his offer, so he turned up the heat a couple notches.

"Aight, you smart little motherfucker," the detective spit the words out of his mouth like a rabid dog. "You think we ran off your customers today, wait until we put a real sweat suit on your building, 24/7. You'll be lucky to make ten dollars a day."

"Yeah, ten dollars a day." The scrawny sergeant yes-manned his partner as he pulled the Explorer up to a red light. Angel turned around in his seat so Fool could get a good look at his intimidation face.

"We'll pick you sonofabitches off one by one until there's nobody left in 714 but old ladies and babies." Angel paused to let that sink in. "And your next ride will end in a dirt nap."

"Yeah, a dirt nap." The sniveling weasel wiped at his nose with a sleeve.

Fool made sure he took his time reacting to their gorilla routine. Angel looked as if his boiling rage was about to explode. Too bad the cops didn't get the response they were looking for.

"Right game, wrong lame." If Fool's hands weren't cuffed behind his back, he would've clapped at the detectives' performance. Instead, he smirked his lips and tried hard not to laugh. "So, you ain't just a crooked cop, you a killa, too?"

No doubt, they could pullover in an alley, put one in his head, and leave his body stinking next to a dumpster, but Fool had to at least make them know for sure that they would bleed, too. He knew Angel was a crook, but he was still no different than all the other cops who came to work and punched a clock every day. They played the games of the streets from nine to five for forty-grand a year and some cushy benefits.

On the other hand, project niggas lived that life day in and day out, no vacation time or sick-leave, and their mentality was always "nothing to lose." Fool knew that the cops knew it too, it was all part of the game, but the twin played for keeps, and if he didn't win, he didn't eat

"You wanna put a sweat suit on our building, you better come dressed in tanks, bullet-proof from head to toe," Fool paused for the effect, and he watched Angel's face as he ripped up the detective's carefully written script and tossed the pieces out the window.

"Cuz I got a gang of more young knuckleheads than Osama had suicide bombers, and they all got itchy trigga fingas. Every time you pop one of mine, one of yours is getting a funeral parade, 21-gun salute." Fool leaned back in his seat, poker-face tight. "So, we ready for combat. What about you?"

No answer came from the front, only silence from Angel and another sniffle from the snotty Weasel. They had both rehearsed their gorilla act, but neither one of them expected the twin to beat on his own chest so hard. After a few awkward seconds, the traffic light turned green, but the Weasel didn't bother stepping on the gas. A horn honked behind them, as if on cue.

"Appreciate the ride." Fool Sat back in his seat and smiled. "Now turn this mothafucka around and drop me back off where you got me."

Duke

# Chapter Sixteen

Creep and Dead Eye were in the middle of a strange game of fetch with a blue rubber ball they found in an alley during one of their dumpster diving trips. The retard bounced the ball off the 10$^{th}$ floor lobby wall. The ball ricocheted back and forth a few times until it finally rolled to a stop. The mangy mutt snatched it up and then took off running down the breezeway as if its tail was on fire.

"Here boy, here boy, here boy." Each time, it took several tries to talk the dog into coming back with the ball.

Creep didn't know what the hell was going on inside his buddy's head. He hardly ever knew what was going on inside his own head, and that moment was a perfect example. He had been struggling with his thoughts all morning, and he kept getting stuck on the difference between right and wrong. Not that he didn't know there was a difference, but which one was which was getting him all mixed up. Most times, when he ran into a predicament that made him choose one over the other, he just went with his gut.

His current dilemma began the other day, right after Monsta made him that offer. At the time, Creep's instincts screamed "Wrong. Wrong." But the green of all those bills twisted his morals into knots. Thoughts of all the things he could do with that much money had him hypnotized. He could buy himself a bus pass and go rummaging through people's garbage all the way out to the suburbs. He could finally eat until he got full. He could even cop a new pair of fake Chucks and a set of markers to turn them into Mike's, and with all kinds of colors.

One of the elevators came to life. The screeching cables and pulley's echoed through the lobby. Dead Eye's tail tapped excitedly against the concrete floor, and its head switched back and forth from the steel doors to Creep as it struggled to figure out which one was more important. The mutt's thoughts got even more confused when the elevator ground to a stop, the door slid open, and then Tameeka and Mini-me stepped out.

Creep's jaw dropped and his eyes popped as he got a close-up of the dark-skinned cutie. A soft cotton T strained against the pointy bulges of her breast, and her blue jean shorts cuffed her hips like two greedy palms. The skin-tight outfit looked as if it were air brushed over her body with blue and white paint, and the sexy combination had the retard's imagination exploding with visions of silky-smooth chocolate syrup poured over thick thighs and tight curves.

"Hey doggy," Mini-me pointed at Dead Eye and smiled as her mother lead her by the hand from the elevator. Tameeka glanced at the odd pair and frowned in disgust before heading in the other direction towards Fool's spot.

The sight of the little girl so excited over seeing Dead Eye turned Creep's X-rated thoughts into warning bells. Once again, his instincts screamed "Wrong. Wrong.. Wrong."

The boy stood there in the lobby, nervous and hesitating. His feet felt like fifty-pound bags of sand, but images of Monsta and his ashy-black fist beating him to a bloody pulp got him moving anyway. He quietly followed the young mother and her daughter down the breezeway.

Every few steps, Mini-me glanced back over her shoulder smiling and waving at the dusty dog. Tameeka only noticed they were being followed when the sun cast Creep's long shadow against the wall in front of her. She picked up her pace, almost dragging Mini-me behind her as they bent the next corner into the dimness of their narrow hallway.

"Doggy," Mini-me pointed only a couple of seconds later.

Then, Tameeka knew for sure the nasty little boy was stalking them. The look of disgust wrinkling her face quickly melted away when the boy and his mutt began inching their way towards them. She turned around, scared, and her small hand fumbled to slide her key into the door lock. Footsteps behind her getting closer made her heart beat wildly. Then she realized the door wasn't even locked, and that made her heart almost stop. There were pry-bar marks on the wood next to the knob.

Tameeka shoved her hand into a pocket.

"Nigga, get the fuck away from us." She spun around thumbing the safety off a black .380 Fool gave her a couple days ago. Creep's eyes bugged out the size of silver dollars, and he threw his hands up in surrender.

"I-I-I- give up."

"Back the fuck up," Tameeka yelled a little louder than she meant to. She had never shot a gun in her life, but that wouldn't stop her from filling the retarded nigga full of holes if he got one step closer.

"Doggy," Mini-me was still stuck on the one-eyed mutt and its frantically wagging tail. Neither one of them knew what the hell was going on.

Creep did, however, but he stood there frozen and staring, not at Tameeka but behind her. They all almost jumped out of their skin from the sound of the door hinges squeaking in the dark hallway. The eerie sound was terrifying, straight out of a scary movie.

A huge shadow snuck into the edge of Tameeka's vision. She spun around with her arm up and finger twitching to start blasting. But before she could find a target, a massive fist flew from the darkness and slammed into the middle of her face. The impact turned her lights out instantly.

Tameeka never felt her nose break, or her body hit the floor, and she didn't even taste the blood and teeth that got knocked loose in her mouth either. Thank God, she was completely deaf to the terrified cries of Mini-me as her tiny hand ripped away from hers.

Monsta bent down, snatched Tameeka's unconscious body into the apartment like a ragdoll, and then started tearing off her clothes. Mini-me's cries and screams filled the hallway, and she didn't know what else to do but follow her mommy inside. Creep had enough sense to step in and close the door. Dead Eye was right behind him, and the mutt ran up to Mini-me and planted a long wet lick across her face.

Creep's eyes were locked on Tameeka. He'd been fantasizing over the gorgeous cutie ever since he spotted her on the ball courts. But the only sex the boy ever had was with the palm of his hand, and he knew damn well he'd probably never get another chance.

Creep gave in to the throbbing pressure slowly building between his legs. For some reason, the blood leaking from Tameeka's swollen lips seemed to increase the lust pumping into the retard's little dick, and he let it grow and grow and grow, until finally, it strained against his pants and threatened to bust out of his zipper.

The boy dropped the rubber ball with one hand, his pants with the other. At first he wasn't sure where his dick was supposed to go, but Monsta stepped in and showed him the way. His instincts did the rest.

## Chapter Seventeen

Angel was extremely disappointed in Run Thang's claim that Fool was no threat. He had shaken off the detective's threats proving that, like his twin, he didn't spook easy either. But, no matter, since the intimidation tactic was only the first stage of Angel's plan anyway. He believed the key to making Fool see things his way was to narrow his options.

Ever since Fool's feet touched down in Cabrini, S.I.U. had kept a squad following him every step of the way. They quickly found out about his spots inside of 624, including the Bucktown hideout. They even got close enough to compliment him on his taste in women, with extra props for the sexy caramel-skinned stunner he had just met at the McDonalds. Most importantly though, the surveillance crew were creeping in his blind spots every time he made a drop.

It didn't take long for S.I.U. to get Fool's daily routine mapped out, and their patience paid off big time just the other day. They were following along during one of his trips through the west-end of a neighborhood called Humboldt Park, and they watched as he met up with a money-green Audi A-6 in a strip mall parking lot. A quick run on the plates gave them their first lead on a "who", and next all they needed were the "wheres" and "whens."

But the Park was a warzone just as violent as Cabrini, and surveillance was always tricky. Plus, the amount of drugs and money that changed hands day in and day out meant there would be an S.I.U. crew checking it in. Running operations through a rival crew's district was the same as stepping on their toes with steel-toed boots.

So, Angel was forced to fall back while Captain McMassey put in a few calls, greased the right palms, and had some local cops put the squeeze on the street-level pushers until they were finally clued-in on where Loco was laying his head at night. From there, it was just a matter of time before they caught the connect slipping.

Meanwhile, Fool wasn't the only mastermind thinking two moves ahead of the game. While the twin was coaching Knuck and WahLah from the sidelines, Angel was eavesdropping on his play-calling. The captain pulled another rabbit out of his hat with some bogus evidence, got a judge to sign his name on a warrant, and a quick call to Virgin Mobile got the crew tapped into Fool's phone.

In spite of what most niggas believed, using a prepaid to do business didn't mean shit to a dirty cop. And while the twin was laying down his daily operations, getting his own crew clicking like clockwork, Angel was listening in and taking notes. The detective even intercepted the texts back and forth as Fool helped WahLah improve on his business model, until eventually, they were milking the Goldmine like a giant titty.

Eavesdropping was just one of S.I.U.'s filthy underhanded tactics. While Angel and the Weasel were dropping Fool off back in Gangsta City, Loco was being boxed-in from all sides in Humboldt Park. Later that evening, the twin was scheduled to pick up a new order, and Angel was tuned-in with his crew on standby ready to make an interception. The big detective was just about to pull his trick-play when Run Thang decided to throw a monkey wrench in his game plan.

A few moments ago, S.I.U. intercepted a text from Knuck, 9-1-1. Fool called to see what the emergency was, and cuz dropped the bad news bomb about Tameeka. A neighbor had heard Mini-me screaming, and when the police arrived, they found Tameeka lying on the floor inside their apartment barely breathing. The ambulance had just scooped her.

The detective began fitting pieces to the puzzle right away, and he quickly figured that his hardheaded partner had to be behind the lunacy. Angel did his homework on Run Thang long before offering him a spot on their team, and he knew all about the reason for the brothers' bad blood. Just the fact that Fool was putting a big dent in their bottom-line was enough reason for a war, but seeing him running around with a new sexy star had Run's jealousy on ten. Angel also knew that his partner held onto grudges with a grip tighter than crazy glue, but the twin wouldn't have gotten his hands dirty with that kind of wet work. So, that left Monsta as the usual suspect.

Angel knew if he could figure that out, then so could Fool, who also had his own goons. That fact had the cop burning rubber back to the projects with a water hose to put out a fire, and he had a bad feeling shit was about to get real hot in Gangsta City. Time wasn't on the detective's side though, and if he didn't quickly get a handle on the current mess, McMassey might just call in someone else to pick up his slack.

Duke

## Chapter Eighteen

Robbie might've been a rookie, but her head-game was all-pro, and her dick tricks earned her another invite to the Groupie Lounge for one of Run Thang's Halloween parties. The twin loved to treat his tricks, and he kept shorty's bag filled with all kinds of pill-candy.

Red was on location as well, and earlier, she tried talking everyone's ears off, so Run had to slip a Z in with an X just to shut her the fuck up. Then he tenderized her ass with a good pounding until she was finally stretched out on the couch, legs half-cocked and all fucked-out.

While the twin exercised Robbie's throat in the Lay-Z-Boy, Monsta was playing director behind one of the cameras. He had all the big-screens around the room lit up with the youngster's head bobbing and dick sucking.

"Gangsta, tighten the focus on these lips." Run helped with the script.

The twin did his own pill popping of course, and he knocked back a Viagra that had his dick feeling like it was in a game of tug-of-war, Robbie's lips versus the little blue pill, back and forth, in and out. At the moment, he felt like a rocket ready to take flight, and he was on the verge of blasting off in the rookie's mouth. He was just about to grab the back of her head and start tapping on her gag reflex when a sudden pounding on the front door interrupted his rhythm.

Bam. Bam. Bam. The pounding sounded just like a police knock.

"Who the fuck is it?" Run shouted without breaking his grip on the back of Robbie's head.

"Po-motha-fuckin-lice," Angel hollered right back.

Without pressing pause, or bothering to get decent for his visitor, Run Thang motioned for his flunky to open the door. The rookie kept up the good work on her knees, and Red continued her trip floating somewhere through the galaxy.

Angel pushed past Monsta with a furious frown creasing his ugly face, but the site of the fuck-party stopped him dead in his tracks and made him momentarily forget what was on his mind.

"Been blowing up your phone," the detective finally got out the words once he regained his composure.

Run nodded down at Robbie and shrugged his shoulders, "Been Busy."

"Ya'll have something to do with what happened over in 624?" Angel didn't want to throw out details in front of company, but the look on his partner's face answered the question with no need to elaborate.

"Watta bout it?" Monsta was too stupid to keep his mouth shut, or stay in his place, but Angel talked around him anyway.

"She'll be pointing fingers when the doctors wake her up, and somebody was dumb enough to leave DNA everywhere." The big cop eyed the flunky sideways, and he let him know how he felt about it. "Stupid nigga."

"Bitch supose' to be dead," Monsta stepped up, chest poked out and ready to go into gorilla-mode, but he ran into something he wasn't expecting.

"Take that bass outta your voice, bitch." Angel chopped the youngster in the throat with a right hand, ducked down and gutted him with a left, and then slick-legged him with a quick swipe of a foot. Monsta crashed to the floor with the impact of an eighteen-wheeler rolling over into a ditch.

The sudden excitement sent Robbie squealing in surprise. Red started moaning and groaning as if she was coming out of her nod. So far, Run Thang wasn't impressed, but Angel wasn't done yet, and before Monsta could recover, the cop was on top of him.

"Told-yo-punkass," Angel punctuated his words with his fists, "about-that-mouth." The camera fell to the floor the same time Monsta did, and it framed a shot of him stretched out across the big-screen like a lopsided UFC title fight.

Once the flunky was completely limp, eyes rolled to the backs of their sockets, Angel stood up breathing hard. He stared over at his partner, who stared right back, still not impressed.

"That shit you pulled will start a war." The cop was running out of warnings, but he reeled in his cool and kept his focus. "Money is too tight already, and ain't no room for jealousy."

"Already gotta fall guy," Run Thang threw his partner a bone for reassurance. "A lil retarded creep."

"Right now, we have some other business to attend to."

Angel gave a look of no bullshit. "Leave your stunt dummy here and meet me in the car."

Monsta was starting to come around as the cop spun towards the door, and before he stepped out, he hacked up a googob and spit it in the flunky's face. He slammed the door on the way out.

Run didn't need more than a few seconds to recover from the interruption. He reached up, twisted his fingers through Robbie's extensions, and then pulled her head back down. The rookie's knees hit the floor and she stared up with her pretty eyes ready to please like a six-month-old puppy. Her face might not have been worth a nickel, but the motor behind her lips would make her a dime-piece any day of the week. Run Thang jabbed the back of her throat.

"Ack-uck-Ack…"

Monsta stumbled to his feet and struggled to stop the room from spinning. At least he was too punch-drunk to be embarrassed.

"Nigga, you still want these leftovers," Run nodded over at cutie Red. "Or you too dizzy to fuck?" The twin felt a little pity for the youngster's pride, so he decided to let him take the new chick for a spin around the block.

Before Monsta was knocked the fuck out, he popped a Viagra with an X, and while he was stretched across the floor, his dick was stretched between his legs. The pill cocktail, along with the pervert in his nature, helped him shake off the dizziness of that ass kicking and led him over to the sexy half-breed, one of the finest scraps Run had ever tossed his way. He'd be damned if a few bumps and bruises stopped him from shredding the girl's pussy to pieces.

# Chapter Nineteen

"Dark-green Audi, north-bound," a call crackled over Angel's radio. "Everyone stay low in case he circles the block." The detective watched as Loco circled twice, just like he thought, predictable.

Angel sat behind the wheel of a plain-Jane Ford Taurus, beat-up and rusty, with Run Thang leaning low in the passenger seat. Parked on a narrow side street in Humboldt Park, they were blending in perfectly with other cars crowding the block. The clock was ticking past 10:00pm, and the crooked cop was itching to call another trick play.

Dotting I's and crossing T's was how Angel got bumped up from wearing a rookie uniform in a patrol car to sporting suits and riding undercover. But doing good detective work didn't have a damn thing to do with how he got his spot in S.I.U. When he was just a regular street cop, his skills in armed-robbery, home invasion, and kidnapping got him noticed by the right people in the right places.

Back then, McMassey was always on the lookout for new talent, specifically, someone good at kicking down doors. Angel turned out to be one of the best, and at the time, he ran with a squad that had a reputation so mean that they had a name, The Body Snatchers.

After the captain found out where Loco liked to lay his head most nights of the week, Angel put in a few calls to bring his old team out of retirement for another hit. Getting the Puerto Rican fitted in a suit of duct tape and tossed in a trunk would be no problem for the seasoned vets.

LaLa was the first Body Snatcher to get Angel's page, and she was also an ex-girlfriend. She got her nametag from a reputation for rocking niggas to sleep, one they would never wake up from. Plus, she was a beast who could handle herself even in the grimiest streets.

Ex drug dealer turned cop turned back to drug dealing, LaLa had the type of personality that made most people judge the cover of her book the wrong way every time they tried to read her. For the Body Snatchers, Tasers and tranquilizer darts were the tools of her trade, and torture happened to be one of her specialties.

Next on the team was Killa, and his name was self-explanatory. He found his way into the Chicago police force way back during the first war in Iraq, right after he got kicked out of the Marines for shooting everything in sight, including women, kids, dogs, and camels. If it moved, it got shot.

A big Dominican named Carmelo brought up the rear of their goon squad. He was a brute the size of a moose, and just about as pretty. He specialized in the heavy-handed tactics that were hard to come by.

The last time Carmelo was on a mission with the crew, they were paid to snatch up a Cartel boss who was hiding out on the south side. Problem was, their mark had barricaded himself inside a safe house with a pack of pits the size of horses, and his body guards were armed to the teeth.

The team had stalled on ideas to flush the man out, so the big Dominican took the matter into his own hands. He drove a Hummer through the safe house living room and tossed a couple of flash-bangs before letting off a few rounds. A couple minutes later-after getting bit by one of the dogs and biting the dog back, he walked out with the vic slung over his back hog-tied with phone cords.

"Audi comin' up behind you," LaLa sent the latest heads up to the crew.

Angel gave her a "10-4" then checked his rear-view. He leaned back in the bucket seat as a pair of sharp blue-tinted headlights crept past their position.

Loco was a local heavy, and he didn't get that fat by being stupid. The P.R. knew his neighborhood like the back of his hand; anything out of the ordinary, and reinforcements were a phone call away. His survival instincts meant staying on his P's and Q's at all times and never getting caught slipping, at least not easily. But

Angel peeped a crack in Loco's armor, and the Body Snatchers were tucked into positions he wouldn't see until it was too late.

The goal of Angel's latest operation was to make their victim believe everything really was what it really wasn't. During the first phase, Run Thang played the part of Fool, and the script called for the twin to act as if he was greedy enough to step on his own connects neck as his next step up the ladder to success. The impersonation of Fool was the easy part.

The second phase called for making Run Thang believe the plan was really about getting Loco doing their dirty work, which was to get rid of Fool once and for all. Painting both of those illusions at the same time was the tricky part.

Directly across the street from the Puerto Rican's house was a four-story walk-up where Killa sat in a second-floor hallway, lights out, holding a sniper rifle behind a window with a good view up and down the block. Carmelo and LaLa were in the street ducking behind parked cars, bumper to bumper and shadow to shadow, staying close but out of sight.

"Make it happen and make it quick," the detective called the shot just as the money-green Audi slid into a parking slot.

Music died down inside the car and the tinted windows went up. Loco opened his door and the interior lights showed that he was riding solo. He stepped out gripping a bottle of Jose Cuervo with a grape Swisher stuck between his lips. A foot kicked the door shut and the alarm chirped. Then he got shot in the ass with 80,000 volts from LaLa's Taser.

"Uh-uh-uh…" Loco tried to shout, but his voice, along with his entire body, was on lockdown by the electricity. His keys jingled to the ground and the bottle of tequila shattered in the street.

Carmelo ran up just in time to catch the P.R.'s body. LaLa laid off the Taser's trigger and scooped his remote. She spotted his house keys on the chain then turned towards Angel with a thumbs-up. After dragging their victim to the front door, her and the big

Dominican disappeared with him inside. Start to finish, thirty seconds flat.

The rumble of an el train rolling along tracks nearby muffled the sound of a dog's angry bark. Angel and Run Thang could barely pick up a woman's high-pitched screams, and other shouts, but all sounds were quickly cut off when the inside of the house lit up with silenced gunfire. From the outside looking in, it could've been a photo shoot, except the camera flashes were popping-off room by room, six, seven, eight times.

Homework gave the detective a rough estimate of how many people would be inside, but that didn't include dogs. Either way, the team knew how to make a clean sweep of the house, and they weren't leaving any witnesses, man or animal.

At the same time Angel was overseeing the operation, McMassey was back at headquarters monitoring 9-1-1 traffic, just in case a nosy neighbor yelled for help. So far, so good, and after a couple of intense minutes, an "all clear" came over the radio.

"Make it good, but don't over-do it." Angel gave Run Thang his cue.

"No doubt, Nigga bout to meet the ugly side of Fool." The twin hopped out of the dusty Taurus. A black hoodie pulled up and tied tight blocked the view of anyone who might've been eyeballing him from a window. Right before he stepped into the crime scene, he dialed his partner's number and put his phone on speaker.

The script Angel wrote was simple and easy to follow, and Run Thang didn't need to put on an Oscar-winning performance. He just needed to look the part, and leave the wet work to Carmelo and LaLa. Even so, the detective wanted to tune in to the action, because he knew better than to underestimate anyone. Stupid niggas didn't last long enough in life to become heavies, not in real life anyway. When Run Thang made Loco believe he was seeing Fool's face, he would start thinking like a dead man with nothing to lose. Angel knew the P.R. would have no reason to cooperate, since they meant to kill him anyway, and the longer he held his tongue, the longer he'd live.

Too bad for Loco, LaLa wasn't just a technician with her torture tactics, she also got her kicks-off during her work. LaLa broke down the science of inflicting pain into three easy-to-follow steps that never failed to loosen lips and make a nigga sink his own ship. Step One: the old fashioned pistol whipping was still a trusty way of making a victim know shit was serious, no joke. Talking was the only way to get out of a jam like that, and the smartest victims talked fast.

Step Two: for the die-hards who thought they were tougher than lizard skin, LaLa forced them into predicaments with even tougher choices – drugs and money, or your mama's life? Maybe wifey and daughter, too? There weren't many gorillas tough enough to watch moms or baby girl being worked on with a pair of pliers and a hammer.

Step Three: even cold-hearts with no love for anybody were scared to death of fire. The key to barbecuing one of those cold-blooded bastards was making him feel it without passing out or dying too quickly. Slow-roasting a hand or foot so they could watch it sizzle and pop was usually enough. But, for the Rambo types who could stand a lot of pain, LaLa made them imagine a life without their manhood. A pair of gasoline boxers made men spill their guts faster than ExLax.

When Run Thang walked into the house, the Body Snatchers already had their victim tied up in the basement so his screams wouldn't carry too far outside. As soon as Loco got a good look at the twin's face, his eyes lit up.

"Aww, Fool, man, what the…" He didn't get a chance to finish. LaLa demonstrated step one with a heavy four-nickel smack across Loco's mouth that turned his front teeth into crumbs.

"Drugs and money."

"You ain't gotta do this," Desperation made the connect talk through the pain and blood. "We can work something out."

"This ain't ebay, mothafucka. Drugs and money."

The Puerto Rican was hurting badly, but time wasn't on the Body Snatcher's side. Since LaLa and Carmelo already killed everyone inside the house, the script was fast-forwarded straight to step three. LaLa stepped up with a bottle of lighter fluid and started soaking a foot.

"No-no-no." Loco was definitely a smart victim. "What'chu want, drugs, money, cars, bitches? I got'chu!" He quickly gave up a stash spot holding a few bricks on the north side.

LaLa soaked his other foot, and she quickly got the safe house holding his piggy bank in the suburbs, but none of the crooked cops were dumb enough to believe Loco was telling the whole truth and nothing but the truth. What he gave up so far was just the top of the iceberg, and he knew they knew.

Angel relayed the info to McMassey, who had another squad on standby ready to locate and rush the connect's stashes with fake warrants. After a few more painful minutes of interrogation, the Body Snatchers packaged their vic in duct tape and relocated him to the trunk of his Audi.

Next, the team bent a few corners while reading from Angel's carefully written script, making Loco believe he was about to go diving for clams on the bottom of Lake Michigan with no scuba gear. But the detective also penned in a plot twist to pull the connect deeper into their illusion.

After riding around long enough to give the captain's other crew time to kick down some doors, a squad car entered the flick and pulled a traffic stop on the Audi. Of course, the Body Snatchers resisted arrest, and they high-speed chased it to make the final scene believable. They hit corners and alleys doing 50, tossing Loco around in the trunk like he was on tumble dry. The finish line was back in Gangsta City where they finally jumped out and disappeared inside one of the buildings.

Saved by the police in the nick of time, Loco crawled out of the trunk bruised, bleeding, and busted up, but he still felt like the luckiest man in the world. He would hold his tongue though, no pressing charges, but he wouldn't hesitate to relay the night's events back to El Jefe and their own crew. Once Loco got a chance to mourn the tragic deaths of his family, and shake off those nightmares, he would chalk-up his losses to the game, and then come at Fool's head with everything he had left.

Surrounded by enemies on all sides, with no decent connect to keep up with his competition, Fool would have no choice but to fold his hand. At least that was what Angel bet all his chips on, and he calculated the odds with more precision than Las Vegas.

Duke

# Chapter Twenty

Fool usually kept a tight leash on his temper, but the last time he saw so much red was six years ago when a jury found him guilty of a murder he didn't commit.

Hours after being found barely breathing in their apartment, Tameeka still hadn't regained consciousness. Her family arrived at the hospital in bunches, and they packed her room shoulder to shoulder. Fool couldn't look her mom in the face. He didn't know what to say. He should've known better than to bring his girl into a warzone.

Sundae met up with him at the hospital, and she watched him wear a hole in the floor pacing back and forth as his mind raced with thoughts of who, when, and why. He had already told her about the early morning ambush on the Goldmine, and Angel's threats. The sexy detective didn't feel comfortable talking in front of so many people, so they moved their conversation to a cafeteria.

"You have to keep your focus, eye on the ball." She tried lowering the boiling point of Fool's temper down to a simmer so he could think straight, no mistakes. The current situation was all bad, but reacting too fast would only make it worse.

"Ain't many niggas dumb enough to try me like this." Fool knew whoever pulled that stunt on Tameeka was someone who could get in and out of the Carter without raising eyebrows. His phone vibrated in his hand, boxing gloves on the caller I.D.

"What's the deal?" he answered on the speaker so Sundae could tune in.

"Streets is screamin' that nigga Monsta," Knuck updated cuz on what he had been hearing so far. "Couple of the guys shootin' dice in the lobby say they peeped him creeping through the building around that time."

"Is he a regular?" Fool wasn't all that familiar with Run's flunky, and for all he knew, the youngster could have family in the building, or other reasons for being over there.

"Naw, that nigga don't fit in our crowd." The Carter was Knuck's domain, and he would never roll out the welcome mat for anyone in Run's crew.

"Good lookin'. But keep that info under your hat in case we gotta use it." Fool wouldn't point fingers until Tameeka woke up and started talking, but he would still make his list of suspects. Knowing his brother's jealousy, and the crooked cop's filthy nature, Monsta was going directly to the top.

"This doesn't sound like Angel's dirty work," Sundae was reading Fool's mind, again. "If it was, Tameeka would've been found dead, or never found at all."

Sundae exposed more of her crooked counterpart's intimidation tactics, showing the method behind his madness. Angel was no doubt tapped into Fools phone, and he probably even had eyes in the hospital right at that moment. She advised the twin to ditch his cell for a new line, find another address to lay his head, and reroute all of his routines ASAP.

"I'll garage the Caddy for another whip, low-key." Fool knew exactly what to do. Back in the days, he used to change cars like clothes. Cheap traps were still plentiful in the hood, and he wouldn't have any problems locating a few buckets. His phone blew up with a green cobra on the caller I.D.

"Say it ain't so?" El Jefe's voice was low and slow, but the anger in his words vibrated through the phone as if he shouted. Word got back to the joint as fast as Loco got back to Humboldt Park.

The old Cobra broke the news about his mans, and it blew the twin's wig back like an atomic bomb. It took Fool several tries, but eventually, he convinced Tuffy that he was in the dark on what went down.

"Run Thang must be desperate." Fool had scooped Tuffy to the animosity between him and twin a long time ago.

"And he gots some thirsty cops pulling his strings." Fool quickly ran down the short version of his recent drama without going into too many details over the phone.

"You gotta clean up that mess, and don't splash no more dirt on me and my people." Tuffy recognized a Gangsta's true colors, and he didn't assume shit. He would give Fool the benefit of the doubt. But at the same time, Loco was itching to bust his guns, and El Jefe's word was the only thing making the Puerto Ricans hold tight to their ammo.

Sundae elbowed Fool with a reminder that Angel was most likely listening in on their conversation, and he would no doubt scramble to find out who Tuffy was. Fool took her warning as his cue.

"Give me a couple days to put all the pieces together. My word, papa, I'll make this shit right." Fool disconnected and looked towards his gorgeous partner for more advice.

"Seems like they're trying to box you in from every angle, and then hit you with everything they got." The strategy of using pawns to put a connect in check was nothing new to Sundae. If Angel could axe the source, and pull the twins into a war at the same time, Fool's options would narrow enough to force him onto the winning team.

Sundae had an idea how they could make Angel's plan backfire in his crooked face. In the meantime, while they straightened shit out with Tuffy, they could tap into her own pipelines.

"We have to hit them all at once, on all sides, so they can't duck what's coming." Sundae clued-in Fool on some of the homework she'd been doing lately.

McMassey and his crew mostly depended on Sgt. Basile's interceptions at the evidence lockup. When she dug a little deeper into the weasel's background, she found out he had a weakness that they could easily exploit, and it was in his pants.

"Men or Women?" Dealing with tricks was nothing new to Fool. After all, his brother was one of the trickiest.

"Girls, and the younger the better. He likes to powder his nose, too." Sundae had more scoops than Ben & Jerry's. She was sure that's how the captain kept his hold on the Weasel.

"So all we gotta do is get a better grip on 'im." Even though Fool never participated in the P game, sicking bad bitches on thirsty niggas was a tactic so old in the hood they gave it a name, "Hoodwinked."

"Exactly, and I gotta treat that no pervert could resist." Sundae had a few other resources she could tap into, and she knew a piece of candy that could ache the shit out of any trick's sweet tooth.

Speaking of tricks, Sundae believed they should make Angel think Fool was finally giving in to the pressure. That would slow McMassey's crew down while they set their own trap.

"Let Angel know you'll meet him halfway on his offer. If they get rid of Run Thang and his flunky, you'll roll out the welcome mat in Gangsta City."

"Aight." Fool caught on quickly. "We can use Monsta's stunt as the reason for the change of heart."

"Yeah, and the smell of jealousy will keep him off the real scent," Sundae agreed. Angel had a knack for recognizing traps, so they needed the details to camouflage it.

Fool couldn't wait to crash-test that dummy Monsta, and in the meantime, they could kill another bird with the same stone. He bounced his plan at Sundae for her input. He could plant a bug in Run Thang's ear about Angel's plan to double-cross him. That would turn them against each other.

Sundae liked it, but before they could call the first play, they needed to put the rest of their team onto the field.

"Use your own crew to get on defense, and don't forget to keep your cool." Then Sundae picked Fool's brain for a little more info on his twin.

"Run's a sucker for a pretty face, but it ain't easy to out-slick a snake." He gave her the skinny on Run Thang's freaky nature, and his violent mentality.

"Don't worry, I know how to trap a trick like him." Sundae started working her phone. Payback was a bitch, and she had the right bitch to pay it back.

Duke

# Chapter Twenty-One

People only had Sgt. Basile half-way figured out. Powdering his nose wasn't the only way he liked to indulge, or even his favorite. Truth be told, the Weasel had never met a drug he didn't like, and whether it got smoked, popped, or snorted, either way didn't make a bit of difference to him. And, most of the time, he overdid it until he was zooted and paranoid, just like he was right at that moment.

On his way to work, and before making his usual stop for coffee and doughnuts, he inhaled two monster lines of coke cut with a crushed Xanax bar. Less than thirty-minutes later, he stood inside of a Dunkin Donuts speedballing with his nose numb and running, and he couldn't shake the feeling that everyone inside was staring at him.

"A box of glazed, and a large Cappuccino, extra cream and sugar, extra cocoa. What the hell, extra everything."

The young Pakistani-looking woman ringing him up seemed to stare at him for a few seconds too long. It made him wonder if he had something on the tip of his nose. Looking around, the Weasel spotted a shiny knob at the end of the handrail keeping customers in line, and he bent down to check his reflection. His nose was the usual irritated-red, eyes bloodshot and twitchy, but everything was normal, no cocaine or boogers.

"Sir, your order," the cashier slid the box of doughnuts and his coffee across the counter, and then looked up at him again.

The sergeant wanted to scream, "What are you looking at?" Instead, he bit down on his tongue, grabbed his order, and then spun around towards the door constantly looking over his shoulder every step of the way. The powder he had been sucking up like a vacuum had his mind wired, and everyone was a suspect.

At the door, he did a 180, neck jerking left and right as he backed out making sure none of the nosy people were following him.

Suddenly, the Weasel felt the glass door bump into something hard behind him. A loud "Ow" made him spin around just in time to see a heavy stack of papers, books, pens, and a red lollipop flying up into the air. It all rained back down to the sidewalk and landed at the feet of a surprised teenage girl.

"Oh. Sorry, sorry, sorry," the Weasel reacted without thinking. He laid his box and cup on the ground then fumbled to help the girl recover what he made her drop.

"I shoulda been lookin'…" His words trailed off into a low mumble as he got a closer look. The girl was sporting a teenie-bopper outfit, a creased white top matched a short checkerboard skirt that showed off bare legs, a typical Catholic school uniform. Waves of sandy-brown hair framed her pretty face, and before the Weasel could stop himself, he reached out and brushed a few stray locks with a finger. The girl's green Now & Later-stained lips cracked a smile at the attention.

"Thanks for helping me." Her voice was soft and sweet. She stood up gripping all of her stuff.

The sergeant estimated that the girl stood barely five-three, and she was probably a sophomore, maybe a junior.

"Ah-hmm," He cleared his throat before trying to respond, but he stalled when the girl's smile disappeared as she glanced at something behind him.

"Shoot, I missed my bus." She pouted her lips and stomped a foot with one hand on a hip.

The drugged-out cop didn't even notice that there was no bus in sight. His filthy mind was stuck on one thing.

"I can give you a ride?" He jumped at the opportunity, but a shadow of disappointment hung over his offer as her eyes darkened with suspicion.

"I'm a cop," he announced before she could say no, and then tugged at the badge clipped to his belt. "And I can get you to school faster than any bus."

"Well," she seemed to relax a little bit. "Okay, but it's pretty far."

"No Problem." The Weasel would've driven her to Alaska if that was how far she needed to go. Instantly, he went from feeling paranoid to lucky as hell. Then he switched on his school-boy act and offered to carry her books.

Inside the blacked-out Explorer, the girl reshuffled her papers to get them organized the way she had them. To the Weasel, she smelled like cotton candy and shower to shower.

"So, what's your name?" He eased his way into her confidence with small talk, mostly the simple stuff. Traffic was light, but he drove slow, taking his time.

"Dominque. You?" She twisted around in her seat, facing him, as the S.U.V slowed for a red light.

"You can call me Anthony." He glanced her way. "I'm a sergeant from…" The end of his sentence got lost somewhere on the tip of his tongue.

The way Dominique sat sideways in her seat, one leg tucked beneath her, had bunched up the checker board skirt high up on her thighs. The twisted position gave the Weasel a quick glimpse of a hairless kitty, and the cameo instantly got his pulse pounding between his legs.

Dominique didn't seem to notice the wardrobe malfunction. A car honked behind them when the light turned green, making the sergeant look up as he hit the gas. He quickly tried to sneak another peep at the girl's pretty slit before it could duck back under her skirt, but to his disappointment, the scene between Dominique's thighs had already shifted, and the view was hidden behind one of her hands.

The weasel shook his head tweaking on some Elmer Fudd shit. He was wondering if he really "saw dat putty cat." He shifted his small talk to corny jokes, hoping to get her even more comfortable.

Dominique fed into his act with an innocent laugh that was almost musical behind her sweet smile. She gradually pulled her guard down and began telling him about herself, where she was from, what school she went to, and how she didn't like the boys her own age.

"Are you a junior?" The Weasel tried to size up her age.

Dominique shook her head, and then pulled out the sucker she dropped earlier when he bumped into her. It was a cherry BlowPop.

"Sophomore?" he guessed again.

"Nope, freshy." She unwrapped the lollipop and made it disappear behind her Now & Later lips.

The Weasel was tweaking so hard he could barely keep his eyes on the road. He watched the BlowPop dip deep inside of the girl's mouth. His eyes were glued to her sucking and slurping, and with a flick of her wrist, she plopped it from her moist lip, delicious.

Dominique pulled the sucker out and held the juicy red ball an inch in front of her lips, hesitating with a look that seemed to say, "Watch what I can do." Then she tickled the tip with her tongue, licking up and down, all around.

"Oh my god," the Weasel couldn't stop the words from escaping his mouth. He shook his head again, tweaking, as if he was coming out of a dream and still not sure if that shit was real or just another one of his speed-balling fantasies. Imagination was a motherfucker.

After Dominique's tongue tease, time seemed to fly by for the high pervert. He stalled on the gas pedal for as long as he could, hoping for an encore, but eventually realized the curtains were closed on the show. By then, they were rolling up to a high school on the far north side.

Yellow buses packed the parking spaces up and down the block, and parents were patrolling on foot, watching their kids safely into class. The Weasel's instincts knew better than to get caught on someone's radar, or camera, so he pulled the Explorer around the corner, incognito.

"You need a ride home?" The pervert kept his fingers crossed.

Dominique had sucked the BlowPop down to the size of a lemon head. She parked what was left behind a dimpled cheek, and then cracked a smile.

"I get out at 3:30."

"I'll be here at 2:30." Sergeant Basile watched the cute girl jump out and head towards the school. He pulled the Explorer into gear and peeled off, still feeling the excitement straining between his legs. He felt naughty, like he needed a spanking.

As the Weasel bent a corner and aimed the S.U.V towards headquarters, the feeling began to return to his nose. He fumbled around in his pockets for another pill and some more powder.

Duke

# Chapter Twenty-Two

"So, how old are you, really?" Introductions were already made, but Fool still couldn't believe what he was hearing or seeing.

"Twenty-three next month." Surprise, surprise. And, Dominique was really born as Trina, but "Trix" was how most people knew her, "Dirty Trix" by those who knew her well. She was a close cousin of Sundae's, and even had a story similar to the twins'.

Trix's moms was a lily-white chick from a middle-class suburban life before she got lost and turned-out in the projects. She died one night tied up in a basement. Daddy was mommy's pimp, and a low-down dirty nigga at that. Before Trix was old enough to remember, he got his goose cooked in the electric chair for cutting open one of his bitches over a rock and fifteen bucks.

Trix grew up as a welfare baby, but the exact opposite of a Similac child. Instead of being fifteen with a body going on twenty-one, she looked barely out of eighth grade when she was really old enough to graduate college. And compared to Tameeka, who turned heads with hips that she threw around like a heavy weight, Trix barely touched five-five in heels, and with a slim figure that kept her age a guessing game. And even though her baby-face was certainly cute, she couldn't match the dime-quality of Sundae's sassy sex appeal, but she did practice her femininity like a professional, and she got it perfect.

Trix was also a typical project-issued ho, but not to be confused as a hooker, no pimp or drug habits. The only person profiting from her pussy was her. And just as her young looks fooled most people, she used her body better than a chameleon, she could change her colors according to a nigga's fetish or fantasy.

For the average pervert, Trix was a tight little teen who was willing to do anything for daddy, and with tricks that would make them cum before they could get it out of their pants. For men with slightly more morals, they could get a sexy twenty-something who was just the right size to be tossed around like a fuck doll. And for the fat-cats who loved to play sugar daddy, she had that "sunshine" that could make him call wifey and tell her, "Daddy ain't comin home no more."

Sundae and Fool followed Trix's "Dominique" routine from the minute she accidentally-on-purpose bumped into the sergeant, and then across half the north-side of Chicago until they finally pulled up in front of the high school. After scooping her up, they listened as she gave them the details of her act.

"I gave'im a quick peep under this skirt. After my lollipop trick, I thought that lil dick was 'bout to bust." When Trix was being her real self, no act, she sounded like a grown-ass little girl.

"Did you reel him in?" Sundae just wanted to know if the Weasel fell for her jail bait.

"I reeled him in like a tuna. He'll be here at 2:30." Trix had the confidence of a seasoned vet.

Even so, Fool still had a hard time talking to her as if she were a grown woman. Everything about the girl seemed to be an illusion, from the golden glow of her suntanned complexion, to the delicateness of her soft features. Even the color of her eyes had him doing a double-take, and the total package intensified her femininity until it radiated from her body in waves of heat. The twin could imagine the Weasel drooling over her schoolgirl act, because at that moment, she had his taste buds watering like a mothafucka.

While Fool sized up Trix's camouflage, Sundae went over the plan for her date to make sure there were no mix-ups in their communication.

"You gotta make him pullover in a parking lot or alley. Nothing underground or inside where we can't keep our eyes on you." Even though Sundae's script called for a ho, she didn't feel all that comfortable with using her little cousin's body like cheese in a rat trap. "And keep him hooked without letting him really taste that bait."

"Don't worry, cuz," Trix had peeped the Weasel's weakness right away, typical pervert. "Once I give 'im a whiff of this kitty, I'll be pushin' that truck myself."

Sundae laughed, but she wasn't doubting her little cousin's skills one bit.

"All I need you to do is get the sergeant out of his clothes, butt-ass naked." She knew the Weasel would be easy money for a pro like Trix. Once the little head between the perverts' legs got hard, it would quickly take over the thinking for the big head between his shoulders, and his better judgment would go out the window just as fast. "And keep your phone on speaker."

"Aight, my signal to move in will be," Trix hesitated for a second before making up her mind. "Huge cock." To her, stroking a man's ego came as second-nature.

They needed to catch the Weasel with his pants down and his dick in the cookie jar. That would be the moment Sundae sprung her trap. She had a friendly traffic cop on standby, and together they would make him an offer he couldn't refuse. The sergeant could either flip on his bosses downtown, or flip on his stomach for big dick Bob in the pen, and he would be flipping and flopping for a few years.

If all went well, the next time a load worthwhile came through the evidence warehouse, the sergeant's bait and switch would go to Sundae's team instead of Angel's.

The sexy detective turned to Fool. "Don't forget to get that dummy mix ready." To keep the scam rolling with no unwanted suspicion, they had to follow McMassey's lead and keep enough narcotic left in their switcheroo to pass a taste test at the state's crime lab, something around five percent would do. At the same time, Sundae would use the Weasel to double-back on the fat captain with their own shake and bake that they had stepped on.

Fool already knew the deal, and to give them even more time to maneuver, he would give Angel a call with some good news. He would accept the crooked cop's offer, but with one condition: Hand over Run Thang and his flunky.

In the meantime, Fool, Sundae, and Trix all went over their plan again, and again, until they had their timing down like synchronized watches.

# Chapter Twenty-Three

The bell rang at 3:30 sharp, and as soon as the classes let out, kids began pouring through the school doors from all sides like lifers making a prison break. More long yellow school buses lined the streets ready to transport the long-distance students, and volunteer parents stood guard on the lookout for child molesters and creeps just like the Weasel.

True to his nature, Sgt. Basile sat double-parked in a no-zone, hazards flashing, and losing track of how many lines of cocaine had disappeared through his straw. He kept his head low behind the Explorer's tints, no need to set off any alarms from the pervert patrol.

It didn't take the Weasel long to spot Dominique standing a half-block away near a row of parked cars. The afternoon sun had her eyes sparkling gray as she scanned left and right for her ride. When her gaze finally fell across the blacked-out S.U.V, she cheesed a bright smile that lit up the rest of her pretty face. She dashed over and the Weasel opened the door.

"Almost thought you wasn't gonna make it." Dominique hopped in breathing hard from her short run. Something in her look said she would've been very disappointed if he hadn't shown up.

"I'm a man of my word." The Weasel sniffed, wiped his nose, and then returned her smile as he shifted into drive and maneuvered through the after-school rush.

"Besides," he added, "I like you, a lot, and I never lie to somebody I like."

Trix's "Dominique" routine was young and naïve, but the Weasel's game was lame, and she'd heard it a thousand times. She caught his bullshit and tossed it right back.

"Thanx. You seem sooo nice," her words oozed with just the right touch of sugar, enough to make the pervert's imagination sticky. From the corner of her eye, she spotted the Weasel's little prick unwinding in his pants like a spring, and she watched him squeeze his thighs tightly, probably straining not to blow his wad.

They approached a busy intersection backed up with heavy traffic. Trix already sat twisted in her seat, and the sergeant took advantage of the angle to take a quick peep, hoping for another wardrobe malfunction. But at the moment, an American History book covered her goodies.

"Oh, I got something for you." He flipped open the armrest between the seats and pulled out a handful of BlowPops, strawberry, cherry, and grape.

"Oooh, I luv cherry," Trix faked her excitement. She knew he was hooked from her tease earlier, and his eyes were lit up like a hungry puppy begging for a treat.

"Thanx." Trix accepted the suckers, but at the same time, she pulled out one of her own. There was no telling what the thirsty pervert dipped his candy into, and there was no way in hell she was going to be his date-rape victim.

Traffic crawled at a snail's pace and then stopped. Trix decided to use the moment to keep her perverted puppy wagging his tail by throwing him a bone. She took her books and laid them on the floor. Her skirt was already jacked up and riding high on her thighs, just like she planned it. But she kept her legs closed, for the moment. Instead, she began unwrapping her lollipop, taking her time and watching his reaction. Once she spotted the Weasel throbbing behind his zipper, the show really started.

Trix wrapped her lips around the sucker's head, at first slow and gently, and then increasing her suction and speed until eventually, she was sucking on the head of that candy as if she were dying to get at the chewy center.

The Weasel was definitely enjoying the show, and he got a lot of help from his imagination. Of course, in his mind, his dick was the BlowPop, and she was ramming him in and out of her mouth, hard and fast, blowing his sucker with no mercy. In real life, Trix swirled the candy slowly across her lips, leaving a sticky trail over the bottom, and then the top. Her cherry-colored tongue darted from her mouth and smacked the juicy red ball with lick after lick after lick. Then she playfully bit the head with her perfectly white teeth. Her last move made the Weasel's jaw drop, and he began wondering how many of her licks he could take before she got to the center of his own lollipop. Then she blew his imagination wide open when her legs shifted and gave him the peekaboo he had been begging for. The Weasel's mind was caught in a sudden game of tug-of-war, Lucky Lolli vs. Hello Kitty, and his attention constantly switched back and forth from Dominique's mouth to between her legs.

Then he remembered something in his pocket. He reached in and pulled out a handful of loose pills, X's, OC's, Xanax, and a few Viagra.

"X?" He offered politely.

"No thanx." Trix declined, so the Weasel popped one himself.

"Oxy?" He held up a pill to show her it was an 80 mg. She shook her head with a smile, so he popped that one too. What the hell, he figured. He popped one of each, and then shoved the rest back in his pocket.

"Ah-hmm," The Weasel cleared his throat, ready to say something, but horns blowing behind them didn't give him a chance to finish his thought. He took a left turn on green.

The ice was already broken between them, but Trix had the Weasel so flustered, he didn't know how to move the conversation into action, so she helped with a little push.

"My last boyfriend liked to watch me, too."

"Huh?" The sergeant took his eyes off the road long enough to glance her way. "What do ya mean?" A cheesy smile creased his face, giving him the look of a pervert who just got caught peeping through a window.

"My lollipops," she twirled what remained of the sucker around inside of her mouth. "He said something about how I use my lips." She shrugged her shoulders as if it were no big deal.

"I don't blame him. You're sooo good with that sucker." The Weasel wanted more, a lot more. "What else did he like to do?"

"Well." Having the Weasel flustered wasn't good enough for Trix. She was about to blow the perverts wig back. Like a head-shrink with a PhD, she steered his mind straight into the gutter. "We used to meet up every day after school and have sex in my room until granny came home from work."

"Did you suck on him, too?" The Weasel took her bait hook, line, and sinker.

"Yup," Trix nodded her head with a shy smile, keeping just enough bashfulness in her Dominique routine. Then she reeled him all the way in. "He loved to cum in my mouth."

The Weasel shivered in his seat, shocked by his own imagination. If he had any morals left, they would've melted through the head of his dick right then and there. He finally built up the courage to get at what he'd been dying to ask her.

"You mind if I give your little cherry a few licks?"

"You would do that for me?" Trix turned her smile into an O of fake excitement, making her response sound as if he was doing her a favor.

"Of course. I would do anything for you." By then, the speedball pumping in Sgt. Basile's system had him on full charge, and anticipation had his taste buds watering like crazy. He sipped back some of the slob.

"But, since you're a cop, we shouldn't go to the projects." Trix looked around out of the windows with a finger on her lips, pretending to think. "Maybe we could pull over somewhere?"

The Weasel licked his lips and nodded his head in agreement. At that moment, he would've agreed to anything. When he spotted an alley behind a closed-down carwash, he "Ah-hmmed" a couple times to clear his throat.

"How about over there?"

"Okay. But I should call granny first, so she won't worry why I'm late." Trix pulled out her phone and dialed Sundae.

The Weasel whipped into the alley and shutdown the Explorer. Then he dug through a pocket and came up with another handful of pills. What the hell, he figured, one of each should be just enough.

"Granny, I'm running to the polish stand for some cheesy fries. I'll be a little late." Trix pretended to listen for a couple of seconds. "Ok, luv ya." She hit the speaker instead of hanging up, and then laid the phone face-down on the dash.

"You are soo cute. Do boys tell you that all the time?" The Weasel poured on his compliments like condiments.

Trix played like a sponge and soaked them up. Then she twisted all the way around in her seat, back against the door, giving up a straight shot of her pussy, no peeping necessary.

"I show yo mine, you show me yours." A fresh shave and a dab of shea butter lotion had her little cookie looking moist, fresh out of the oven.

The Weasel reached over to pet her kitty, but Trix quickly hid it with a squeeze of her thighs.

"Your turn, silly." She played that off well. There was no way in hell he was sticking his dirty fingers and crummy nails inside of her.

"Okay, Okay." The Weasel's frantic hands fumbled for his zipper. By then, he was struggling not to empty his clip before he could even get his pistol out of the holster. Finally, he pushed his Dockers down to his ankles, and then twisted around in the seat.

At first, Trix didn't see anything, only a pair of wrinkled nuts. She leaned in closer for a better look, and it took a lot of leaning to spot it. The Weasel's package looked like a hairy backpack strapped to a Popsicle stick. A laugh escaped her lips before she could stop it.

"What's so funny?" If the pervert wasn't so high, his feelings would've been hurt.

"What da hell I'm su'posed to do with that?" Trix accidently stepped out of her role.

Only amateurs lost their composure during a date, and normally she would've used her skills to stroke his ego until she had him feeling like Rocky Balboa, the great white hope. If Trix wanted to, she could've even had him beating on his chest like King Kong. But, not that time, though.

"That looks like a baby carrot, and I ain't no damn rabbit." Trix had handled over a hundred dicks in her young career, but she had never seen one so small. It almost made her forget to signal Sundae to move in and pull the curtains on that freak show. But, before she could shout it out, the cocktail of prescriptions suddenly transformed the pervert's common sense into courage.

"Why don't you suck it like that lollipop?" He reached across the seat before Trix could react and grabbed a fistful of her hair, and then he started pulling her head down toward his little pecker. Big mistake.

"Uh-uh," Trix ducked out of his grip with ease, and at the same time, she whipped out a small butterfly knife that seemed to appear in her hand like magic. With a couple flicks of her wrist, the razor-sharp blade swished through the air with sound effects like a Kung Fu flick.

Before the red-nosed Weasel realized that what he just saw wasn't part of his imagination, the knife was buried hilt-deep through the back of his hand and had it pinned to the dashboard's cheap vinyl. He leaned his head back and let loose a scream that could've come straight from an episode of Tom and Jerry.

"Ow-woo-ooh-hoo-oow-woo."

Right on time, the Woop-Woop of a loud siren with bright blue lights flashed behind the Explorer. Trix backed out of the passenger door. The Weasel went into panic-mode and tried to pull the knife out of his hand, but no good, it was stuck. Next, he struggled to pull up his pants but messed around and spilled the rest of his pills all over the floor. Then the driver's side door was snatched open.

"Well, well, well," Sundae stood there shaking her head with a pitiful smile. "You didn't just have your dirty hands in that little girl's cookie jar, did you?"

"It's not what it looks like, I swear. What the fuck?" The Weasel's words choked off at the sight of the detective's gold S.I.U. badge. When he spotted the camera phone rolling in her hand, his heart dropped into his stomach and his pecker shriveled like a wet noodle.

"I-I-I..." The sniveling Weasel felt like a rodent with its tail caught in a rat trap.

Before he could finish stuttering his useless excuse, Sundae cut him off with some bad news. "Sergeant Basile, you work for me now."

Duke

# Chapter Twenty-Four

"You know what they do to child molesters in the joint, don't you? Especially white perverts who like molesting little black girls?" Sundae went in on the sergeant, reading him the riot act, and she didn't sugarcoat any of it.

"Wh-wha-what d-do they do?" The Weasel knew firsthand how easy it was for a crooked cop to arrange a one-way prison trip, no travel agent needed.

"They're going to love sharing your little asshole, passing you back and forth, cell to cell, big dick to big dick."

"I-I-I'm to-too small to g-go to jail." Thoughts of a Mandingo party had the Weasel in full panic-mode. His shitty life flashed before his eyes, and Sundae was promising to make it flash in bright lights, primetime news.

"You can either work for me, or eat dick meat sandwiches three times a day for the next three years." Sundae knew she couldn't box-in the sergeant without giving him a way out; he would clam up to keep his situation from getting worse.

The Weasel switched sides and rolled over on his crew faster than a C.I. for the feds. Turned out, that very night, the captain had a drop set up and ready to go. The sergeant had intercepted a load of seized evidence, two duffel bags in the back of the Explorer, right before he got side tracked by Trix, and he was supposed to meet up with Angel in a few hours to make the hand-off. Sundae had to act fast while Fool and WahLah were in a Goldmine kitchen baking up a batch of bullshit with a new recipe. When Sundae called the twin with the play, they sped up their whip game to get the cakes boxed up in time for the switcheroo. Then Fool pulled Knuck off the bench to play his part, and they needed to keep their offense on the field, two minute drill, no timeouts.

Knuck's first job was getting Run Thang on the line, and then putting a bug in his ear that would get him looking left while Fool and Sundae went right. It was no secret where Knuck kept his loyalty, but the cousins never had a reason to lock horns with each other, so when he reached out, the twin didn't automatically throw his guard up.

"Man, fam, you got that rock star status, name ringin' off the hook." Knuck kicked off the conversation as if he had a line on a bit of juicy gossip, all bad.

"I got fans everywhere." Run had been ducking shots from haters his whole life, so what was new?

"The crooked cop is dragging your name thru the mud like a dead-weight, and he's tryna shake it. Knuck knew his news would make cuz throw up his radar right away, and he was right.

Run's first thought was that the call from Knuck was one of Fool's tactics to feed him some bogus info, to maybe get him off his square and make him slip up for a setup. Eyes on the streets never closed, always watching, and if the opportunity presented itself, a nigga wouldn't hesitate to use a middleman to drop a dime on their competition. The game was cold but fair, and in Gangsta City, snitches didn't get stitches. They got two to the head, one for the lesson, one for the message.

Even so, Run Thang couldn't deny that he'd been feeling the tension between himself and his partners. He didn't trust any of the crooked cops as far as he could see them, and playing with Angel was like playing with fire. Run wouldn't put shit past that dirty mothafucka.

Of course, Knuck already knew cuz wouldn't just take his word for face-value, so to make the script more believable, him and Fool kept the lines simple, and something like a true story but with no truth.

"Your partna bout to push you some Jiffy mix to ruin your rep. And the dummy drop is tonight." Sundae's timely info was key to Knuck's act. And while she knew Captain McMassey wouldn't double-check the quality of the sergeant's drop, Fool knew that his brother would.

"Angel is the type to plant bodies, not dummies." Run Thang might not have trusted the crooked cop, but he knew his partner's M.O. was dependable. If Angel was cutting ties, he wouldn't use a smoke screen to do it.

Knuck and Fool knew that would be exactly how Run would think, so they thought one move ahead of his, with a couple more moves to back that one up just in case.

"Your partna fucked up some money trickin' off wit those rats. Now, he's playin' the blame game, and he needs a fall guy for that fat-ass captain.

Information on Captain McMassey was kept strictly top Secret, G4 classified, and that was all Knuck needed to say to convince Run that the rat was out of the bag.

"So, why you pullin' my coat? You could'a took that info and ran wit it." That was another big difference between the twins. While Fool believed in teamwork, us against them, Run Thang was every man for himself, and everyone was his competition. He would've used that info like a bullet, and kept one in the chamber.

"They tryna cut Fool in while they cutting you out. But cuz is spreading his wings on some other shit." Knuck could almost feel Run on the other end of the line nibbling at his bait.

"And?" Still, the twin hesitated to sink his teeth in. The police weren't the only people Run didn't trust.

"We can tag team that threat. Once we crush 'em, Fool will fall back while we chop up the land, me and you, fitty-fitty." Knuck kept his fingers crossed as he listened through the silence on the line.

Run Thang took his time responding as he weighed his options. He could either keep dancing around a ring with a bunch of crooked-assed cops, or he could get back into a fight with enemies he was familiar with. And with Angel, he'd never know when his usefulness would be considered used up. But with his brother, at least he'd see the punches coming if they got thrown.

"Aight. I'mma taste-test the next drop, see if your info is on point. Either way, I'll get back at 'cha." Run's decision should've been a no-brainer, but he wasn't going to make it look that easy.

"Just stay on your P's and Q's, cuz." Of course, Knuck knew that.

"No doubt." Run's P was a 9mm, his Q was a .40, and he never left home without them.

"Struggle." Knuck killed the line.

# Chapter Twenty-Five

It was a dark night, cloudy with no moon and even darker around the old abandoned junkyard. The last time street lights worked in the area was way back in the 70's. When Run Thang pulled in pushing his Beamer, headlights exposed McMassey's tinted suburban and the two usual Crown Vic's idling in the darkness. He slid the Beamer's chrome blocks into an empty spot and hopped out.

"Your competition is killing us." The fat captain got straight to the point. "Seems like everybody is making money but you."

"You doubtin' my management style?" Run Thang kept his poker-face blank, no worries.

"This look like McDonald's to you?" McMassey frowned as he sucked a piece of Tobacco from between his stained teeth.

"Yeah, this ain't no mothafuckin' McDonalds," the Weasel yes manned. No need to change up his role. That would only make the crew suspicious.

"And having your flunky rape that girl was a bad move. Time to put an end to that nigger's career." Angel used the opportunity to slide that in. It was true, the dummy's stunt would start a war, but that wasn't what worried the cop most. He needed to get Fool on the team, pronto, before the captain pushed him into early retirement.

The whole crew's presence was Run Thang's first indictor that Knuck's word was good as gold. Before cuz tipped his hat, the twin would've went into the drop thinking it was just a routine pickup, not a powwow four-deep. And he was glad he kept his own word to go in strapped, double-breasted, just in case.

"You gotta make up your mind. You want me to put a lock on those profits, but every time I make a move, you callin' a foul." Run wasn't the only one wearing a poker-face, but he could see right through theirs. And he could tell that showing his own hand at the moment would probably get him killed.

"Too much heat." Angel shook his head.

"Yeah, too much heat," The red-nosed Weasel wiped snot on the back of his sleeve.

"Y'all are the mothafuckin' heat." Run Thang watched the fat captain watching him through the rearview.

"We ain't the only heat." Angel was running out of patience.

"Yeah, we ain't the only heat…"

"Shut the fuck up!" So was Mc Massey. "Maybe we should start dealing with your competition instead?"

The S.I.U. captain was familiar with Angel's plan to upgrade to the better twin, but he wasn't in on every single detail. If he was, he wouldn't have just said that. But either way, he was having second thoughts about handing over their newest load. They were putting too much risk into too little profit, and Run seemed as if he was getting a little too comfortable on the throne he built for himself.

"Frank Nitty in 534 has his shit together." McMassey rattled off a few examples. "The Murda Squad over on the Wild-End are making moves, too."

"Midgets to a giant. All of 'em." Run laughed them off.

"What about Fool?" The captain threw the name at Run like a right-cross. He meant to force the twin into seeing his part of their partnership from the only position he fit in, at the bottom with their feet on his neck. But, in reality, all the captain did was make the twin's trigger finger twitch and his hand slide down to his waist.

None of the cops realized how bad Run Thang was itching to up his SIG's and get them popping. He could dome the captain, and maybe even the dirty Weasel before they heard a shot, but then Angel's reaction times probably weren't that slow. Plus, who knew if they had backup lurking somewhere in the background where he couldn't see. And, anyway, he was still trying to figure out who was his worst enemy, his competition or his connects. He kept his cool for the moment.

Angel already tried telling his boss that neither one of the twins would shake so easily. Project mentalities never expected to live past twenty-one, and Run Thang was an old man in his thirties. He threw McMassey a look, warning him not to expose any more of their routine. They needed to finesse something better than their usual spook tactics. The detective gave his captain a quiet nod.

"Pop the rear hatch," McMassey ordered the Weasel to handle his dirty work. Then he turned in his seat so Run could get a good look at his chubby face.

"Get the profits back in the black, or this'll be the last donation to your cause. And you got two days to put that gorilla down before we do." S.I.U. had a whole file cabinet full of unsolved murder, and he wouldn't hesitate to link one to Monsta.

Run Thang's skin might as well have been bullet-proof. He let the threats bounce off like a ricochet. He stared back at Mc McMassey with a blank look that showed the crooked cops just how much they had him sweating, not at all.

The twin hopped out and walked around to the back of the heavy Suburban where the sniveling sergeant was waiting. The Weasel stood between a pair of duffel bags damn near as tall as him.

The pervert didn't have a clue about Angel's plan to bench one twin for the other, or the double-cross between crooked cops, and he was completely in the dark about the fake bricks inside the duffels. All he knew was his face wouldn't be headlining the evening news anytime soon. There would be no trips down-state for dick meat sandwiches, and he was still getting paid either way.

Duke

## Chapter Twenty-Six

On his way back to the high-rise fort in the 30 Block, Run Thang spotted Ghost the dope fiend trying to unload a hot case of baby formula in front of the corner store on Larrabee. Despite the old timer's looks, he had more uses than just boosting, standing on lookout for a crew, or scaring the shit out of kids on their way home from school. Ghost had been banging needles for over thirty years, and when a pusher needed a taste-tester, he was the main go-to guy in the projects. Nobody knew good dope like a good dope fiend, and the old man's resume was written on his body in track marks.

Run slid the Beamer to the curb and interrupted one of the old head's sales pitches.

"Ghost, got yo tools?"

"Like a alley mechanic," Ghost hollered right back. The tools of his trade were needles and cookers, and he never left home without them. He never knew when his motor would need an emergency tune-up. He hobbled over to the driver-side window.

"Throw that bullshit away and get in." Run Thang popped the locks.

Ghost didn't think twice about tossing the formula, and before the case hit the curb, a mob of fiends swooped in like vultures. Thirty seconds later, and the bottles disappeared in every direction.

The twin had to drop the windows just to turn down the dope fiend's stank a few notches. Usually, he wouldn't have let a clucka ride the leather in his whip, but the present circumstances were unusual, and there was no time to make the man walk all the way back to the building.

Run Thang kept a vacant apartment on the 30 Block's top floor where Monsta was already posted inside. The one-bedroom unit used to be one of the twin's stash spots, but he turned it into a shooting gallery for his customers a long time ago.

Inside the tiny front room, a pack of addicts had just got back from shopping, and they were sucking up dirty water in syringes, burning their fixes in bottle caps over matches, and searching for veins in the dim light. The big flunky led the way to the bedroom. His size 15 Nike's kicked at rats and stomped roaches on their way past a drunk who was passed out face-down in a pool of vomit.

Run Thang and his party of three weren't the only people who booked the apartment's VIP suite for the evening. When they slid through the empty doorway, the street light leaking through the window spot lit Vicky the fiend stretched out on top of a filthy mattress with a dusty nigga's ashy black ass pounding his way between her legs. At the same time, another man poked at her neck with a needle. Monsta reached down and snatched him up by his collar before he could tap into one of her veins.

"Take dis bitch in da otha room."

The two dudes hopped up and relocated with no complaints, but Vicky took her time. She knew the twin's freaky reputation well. Back in the day, she used to suck his dick damn near every day, and she was hoping he would let her drop down for a hit.

"Run, can I-" a back-handed slap across her face cut her bid short.

"Bitch, we got bizness!" Monsta's knobby knuckles damn near knocked out one of her teeth.

Run Thang never had patience for a clucker either, and he planted a Jordan print on the back of her ass as she crawled out on hands and knees, dirty jeans clinging around one ankle.

Drama was nothing new to Ghost, and he was already digging through his kit for the right tools to get his job done. He found a cup on the floor with two dead roaches floating on top of some stale coffee. He plunged in his syringe and sucked up enough for a hit.

"Fuck kinda water is that?" There weren't many sights left in the world that could surprise Run Thang, but that was some nasty shit.

"Rain water, toilet water, water is water." Ghost hadn't had a hit since early that morning, and he wasn't feeling all finicky. He sat on the edge of the mattress to steady his hand as he fired the cooker. Monsta and Run stood posted on their feet, not about to touch anything in the room.

Veteran heroin addicts had different techniques for mainlining; some went through their arms, legs, between toes, or even jugulars. But Ghost hadn't seen a vein in one of those spots in years. They all had collapsed. So he had to go searching for blood flow in other parts of his body. At the moment, he had some feeling in his nuts, so he tied them off with a shoestring, and after a few smacks and a couple well placed pinches, he knocked in the plunger before his opportunity disappeared.

Another trick of a dope fiend's trade was getting their heart-rate up. The faster that diesel fluid got to the brain, the harder it would hit. Ghost slipped the knot on the shoestring to give his nuts some breathing room, and then he began rocking back and forth, and flapping his arms like a sick chicken trying to take flight - his version of jumping jacks, without the jumping.

Good dope usually got the fiend's mouthwatering instantly, and he smacked his lips searching for the taste. Run Thang knew the deal, and he patiently tapped a foot while he waited for the verdict.

"Man, Run, you been tap dancin' on this shit, or what?" Ghost wasn't looking too impressed, or all that high either.

"What it taste like?" The twin was starting to get heated.

"Like shoe leather." Ghost never knew Run Thang for stepping on his dope, and he was starting to have serious regrets about tossing that baby formula in the gutter. He could've used that hustle on some real dope.

"Good lookin'," Run pulled a grip from his pocket, peeled off a Grant and tossed it on the floor. Then he leaned his head out of the room until he spotted Vicky digging through a nigga's pocket, the same dude passed out in his own vomit.

"Dig this," He pulled her into the room with a nod. "Suck this nigga's dick, and you can have the rest of that dog food."

Run tossed another bag of bullshit at Ghost for his troubles, and then him and Monsta made their exit. Out on the breezeway, the twin gave his flunky instructions to snatch the fake bricks out of his whip and go donate that shit to the needy. Next, he hit the speed-dial for Knuck.

"What's the deal?" Cuz answered sounding like he was choking on a blunt.

"It's about to be all bad for those crooked cops." Run Thang was pissed the fuck off, and he was ready to get shit cracking - pronto.

## Chapter Twenty-Seven

"He's pulling in now." Fool sent Trix a text to give her a heads-up. He was parked halfway down the block, on the lookout for his brother, while Sundae's little cousin stood posted in front of a small fish joint a few streets over from Gangsta City.

"I'm on it." Trix took her cue and stepped up to the outside order window.

"You order?" A short Korean with a thick accent stood on the other side of the greasy bulletproof glass wearing a grimy apron. Behind him, his wife was chopping heads off of fish with a meat cleaver.

"Gimme a small catfish dinner, suicide sauce with cheesy fries." Trix slid the man a dub. According to Fool, the fish joint was Run Thang's favorite Friday night spot to grab a bite, and he always went for the twelve-piece house special, chopped, fried, and drowned in hot sauce. A Mountain Dew Red washed it down.

Just like clockwork, the twin's box Chevy pulled into the lot, 22-inch rubber crunching gravel, and 15's banging on the truck like they wanted to get out. When the doors popped open, a young pretty chick, light-skinned with long curly hair, exited the passenger side. Run walked up with the girl decorating one of his arms.

It took less than a heartbeat for the couple to spot Trix at the window standing oh-so sexy in a tight mini, cotton-candy-pink, that barely hid the tops of her curvy thighs but hugged her hips with plenty of love. A matching T was like frosting drizzled over a cupcake, and it cut off just in time to show off a cute little bellybutton punctuated with a tiny gold ring.

Trix called the get'up her "Trapper fit," like honey for a bear. The young chameleon's transformation was flawless, from a piece of jail-bait that was irresistible to a pervert, into a young philly that would make any baller want to wife her.

At first, Trix wasn't too sure about what kind of bait to put on her hook that night, since all she really knew about Run's taste was what Fool had told her. But, thankfully, her confidence spiked when the twin started sizing her up like a kid in a candy store, drooling over a Hershey bar, and he wasn't shy about letting her know how much he dug the fit.

"Cutie, you gotta name for that figure?"

"Cheri, you?" Trix wasn't bashful either.

"Damn, that's my favorite flavor." The twin licked his lips as if he could taste it. "You can call me Run."

Trix flashed her dimples, denting her checks with a smile as she struggled to hold her composure and not laugh in the nigga's face. Fool had brought her up to speed on his brother' mentality. He had the ego of an alpha with the passion of a super freak. So they wrote the plot of their script to revolve around the head of his dick.

"Can I take that as a compliment?" She didn't overdo it, though.

"Can I get a pose?" Evidently, blunt was part of Run's personality also.

Trix played along. She side-stepped and poked out a hip so he could get a good look at her back pocket.

"Damn, baby, you can take that talent international, Victoria Secret…" Run poured on his compliments like toppings on a dessert.

Meanwhile, Trix flipped through some mental options for a response. The script called for her to tell him she was a college student, or maybe an intern at a hospital, anything but a project chick. But, like most niggas, she had a feeling he would be intimidated by intelligence, so she skipped that part without dumbing down her act too much. It was better to keep him guessing anyway.

"Baby gurl, you definitely get a dime in my book." The way Run's imagination was stroking her body, Trix wouldn't have hesitated to bet his dime right, double or nothing.

While she kept the twin's focus on her hips, she side-swiped shorty under his arm with a quick glance. The girl was tall and slim with decent curves in all the right places, her complexion was light and bright, and her demeanor was under the influence, probably X. Whatever her drug of choice was, it popped a glassy stare into her brown eyes that had her looking as though her thoughts were stuck on a busy signal.

Fool knew going in that Sundae's little cousin had to come on strong to even get Run's attention. And lucky for the team, special effects was Trix's specialty. She had to make her smoke screen thick, or otherwise, Run would see her act coming from a mile away. Then he'd classify her as a digger and string her along just like the spaced-out cutie.

So, not only did Trix have to convince the twin, she had to reel in her competition as well, like licking two suckers at the same time. When the Korean pounded the greasy glass with a fist and slid her order through the box, she used the opportunity to turn all the way around for another pose that exposed her curves from a better angle.

"Ohh-wee, that ass has more shape than a pear." Run stepped up with one of his favorite moves. He palmed the bottom curve of her ass and squeezed like he was testing the ripeness of a melon in the produce isle.

"You always so bold?" Trix pretended to be impressed with the gorilla's tactics, and the gorilla fell for it.

"I'mma spoiled Gangsta. What I want I take, what I don't I break." Trix didn't respond right away. Instead, she used her body language to tell him it could be his to take, or break. At the same time, she caressed Red with a slow look that made the Suburban cute dizzy. A silly giggle from her sexy lips proved she liked the attention.

"You swing that way?" Run took the bait, and the possibilities had him drooling.

"I like to treat myself sometimes." Trix swiped the screen of her phone. "Gimme yo numba."

Run didn't hesitate to drop his digits, and he only released his grip on her ass when she promised to give him a booty call sooner rather than later. Then Trix cracked the Styrofoam lid on her catfish dinner as she walked away from the restaurant. Down the block, Fool watched from his lookout spot as Sundae's little cousin munched on a cheesy fry while heading west on foot towards a short bridge that crossed a set of train tracks about two streets over. They picked the route because traffic was usually light at that time of night, but police cameras covered every square-inch from damn near every angle. Surveillance was all part of the plan, plus, the route made synchronizing their timing easy.

Just as Trix began crossing over the bridge, Fool fired up the engine on a baby-blue box Chevy that matched his brother's Impala to a T, from the vinyl on the top down to the 22's on the concrete. Sundae helped out with the fake plates to kill any alibi Run might come up with at a trial.

When Trix reached the top of the bridge, Fool slammed on the brakes next to her. He jumped out with sleeves covering his tats, but no mask or hat, so the police cameras could get a clear view of his face.

Somewhere across town, at the city's 9-1-1 call center, Sundae's contacts were monitoring the phones, waiting for an anonymous caller to dial into their hotline. They had to make sure Crime Stoppers got all of the details just right, everything from Run Thang's blue and white Mikes covering his feet, the Murray's shine tightening the waves on top of his head, to the unmistakable swag of his walk.

Fool performed his stunt-work like a pro for the cameras. He walked up to Trix acting like he knew her, and without saying a word, he smacked her with a wide-armed swing that exaggerated his movements. Catfish and cheesy fries flew everywhere. The

Styrofoam tray fell out of her hands and she screamed as if she were trying to win an Oscar. In reality, Fool's hand barely caught the side of her face.

The twin scooped her up, tossed her light weight into the passenger's seat, and then he finished his performance by peeling off before any real eyewitnesses could drive past and notice the commotion. There was no room for heroes in their flick. The fake kidnapping scene was over in less than thirty-seconds, start to finish, and that time there would be no case of mistaken identity.

Duke

# Chapter Twenty-Eight

Run Thang knew it was just a matter of time before Angel started feeling freaky, and he would come around sniffing for some young pussy with his nose wide open. So, when the detective called requesting an appointment with Robbie, the twin figured that would be the perfect opportunity to flip the script on the crooked cop, and give Monsta his shot at a rematch at the same time.

Run gave his flunky the go-ahead to hold Robbie over in the Fab 40 for the pickup, with permission to warm her up while they waited. But, someway-somehow their communication must've gotten crossed up, because the girl had been bugging ever since Monsta brought her up to the twelfth-floor lobby. No doubt, the groupie knew her role, and she wouldn't have hesitated to bust down for Run, or back it up for Angel, but she was stiff-arming the big goon like Adrian Peterson running through a linebacker. Either she didn't get a copy of the night's script, or she just wasn't feeling her role.

Monsta was sure feeling her, though, and what he felt was rock-hard and ready to bust. He stood leaning against a wall by the elevators eyeing shorty as she reclined on the arm of a dusty sofa somebody tossed out, along with a busted table, and a broken lamp stand.

The young star was rocking a pair of red shorts so tight they looked painted on her ass as if by an airbrush. The only light bulb in the lobby buzzed on its last leg but still burned bright enough to make the brown skin of her thick thighs look smoother than milk chocolate on a milky way. Her eye-candy was teasing the shit out of Monsta.

"Cum on, gurl, u ain't got dem pretty lips fo nuttin'." He had been arguing with her for the past ten minutes, and he was starting to run out of patience. He damn sure wasn't going to keep begging, and so he began inching over her way, mean-mugging and ready to dial up his gorilla-mode.

"You need'a pill to get dim jawz luse?" He pulled out a handful of Chanel Bags, double stacks of X, covered in some pocket lint.

"Uh-uh," Robbie rolled her eyes feeling confident. "Run ain't told me I gotta do nobody but Angel."

"See, dat's da muh-fukin' pro'lem." Monsta felt he was being too soft on the rookie.

Run Thang would've just walked up and slid his dick in her mouth without saying a word.Using his boss' moves as inspiration, the flunky reached out to wrap a heavy hand around the back of Robbie's head. But the girl saw his move coming, though, and she bobbed and weaved like Tyson ducking a Holyfield haymaker.

"I ain't putting that dirty thing in my mouth." Robbie puckered up as though she were about to gag from the thought. She only ever sucked the flunky's dick when Run told her to, and the last time she went down on that nigga it tasted like a sour pickle.

"Stop actin' stuck up wit dat mouf." Monsta didn't give a fuck about her taste buds, or her gag reflex. He made another move, that time using his weight to pin her against the arm of the sofa.

"I rather suck a donkey's dick." Robbie tried to get slippery and slide past him, but she was too little too late.

The goon got brutal with a backhand that knocked the girl face-down into the dusty cushions. Her vision instantly went dizzy with shiny stars and colorful rainbows. By the time she shook it off, Monsta was standing over her and reaching through his zipper.

The goon's perverted reputation was no secret, but Robbie knew she belonged to Run Thang, and she never thought the flunky would be dumb enough to damage the boss's property. Robbie thought wrong, though, and if she could've heard the dummy's thoughts at the moment, she would've took off running out of the building, out of Cabrini, and never came back.

Before the girl could get the feeling back in her legs and make a run for it, Monsta snatched her up by her hair and drove his hips in toward her lips. His dirty dick stabbed from the right. Robbie cut to the left. The goon cursed when he missed.

"Bitch." He cocked his hammer back again and tried to get a better aim before firing a second shot. Robbie was too good, though, and she ducked her mouth at the last second, making him skid off a cheek into one of her eyes. Before she could blink back the tears, he knocked her upside the head with it.

"You gonna suck dis da easy way, or da hard way."

It wasn't Robbie's first time getting smacked around, but bullshit ain't about nothing. She kept her lips clamped tighter than a pair of Vise Grips.

Monsta reached for another backhand to get her mind right, but just as he zeroed-in on the right spot to make it hurt the most, the sound of footsteps shuffling behind him stopped his swing mid-flight. He began to spin around, but the metallic sound of something heavy "click-clacked" behind him, and he hesitated. Then he felt the pressure of cold steel pressing on the back of his head.

"Put that piece of shit back in your pants." Angel's voice didn't surprise anybody. Monsta put his wood up and turned around slowly, no sudden moves. Then he locked one of his crooked eyes on the end of a black.40, the other on the cop.

"You gonna take her place? You know how to suck dick?" The big dummy's lips creased in an ugly sneer from his own joke, but nobody laughed.

Angel didn't know the flunky would be there, and his presence smelled like bullshit to the detective. Also, the confidence in Monsta's eyes told him that Run must've put the jumper cables on his crash-test dummy and charged his battery. Angel ignored the small talk and gave the girl her cue.

"Meet me in the car."

That sounded good to Robbie, but getting lost sounded even better. She mashed out down the steps with both feet on the gas, no looking back.

"I told you, try me again, and that would be your last lesson." Angel tightened his finger on the trigger.

The crooked cop didn't get his instincts at the police academy; he got his by grinding in the gutters of the streets. But even with a third eye and a crystal ball, he had no way of knowing exactly how deep he cut into the flunky's pride. The youngster held onto grudges with a grip more obsessive than OCD. Even though his attention span was shorter than a kindergartener's with ADD, he had been itching to get back at Angel ever since he put him on his ass.

To Run Thang, if it didn't make dollars it wasn't his problem, but lucky for his flunky's crushed ego, he found some profit for his pity. The twin finally came through for his boy with a rematch, Ali versus Forman, a rumble in the jungle, except their fight was fixed, and the odds weren't looking good for the champ.

Monsta's gap-toothed smile gave away the plot, and it drew the cop's attention to the sneaky footsteps coming up behind him. Angel began to spin, but a "Click-clack" stopped him from reacting in time. He knew the pull of a magnum's hammer when he heard one, and that sounded like a big one.

"Up the banga befo I turn yo lights out."

Angel didn't need to know Knuck's voice to make him lower his .40, but he craned his neck to have a peek anyway, and he recognized Fool's right-hand man right away.

"Y'all going against the grain on this one?" The crooked cop had always been too big-headed to believe he could be set-up on his own turf. Plus, he figured Run Thang had too much to lose.

"You ain't the grain." Knuck didn't elaborate. And only he knew that Run and Red, at that very moment, were checked in at a casino on the Indiana side of the border with his membership card in rotation on a craps table for an air-tight alibi.

"You a cop killer? You ready for that kind of heat?" Angel played his trump card, one he never thought he'd need, since most people were smart enough to fold a hand like that. Besides, he could tell that his present predicament wasn't a straight hit anyway. If it was, they wouldn't have been talking. He would've been dead already.

Knuck backed up a step to keep his aim straight. That was Monsta's cue, and he took it with a right hook that rocked the cop back on his heels. Angel lost the grip on his .40 and it skidded across the floor out of reach.

The big flunky had that buttermilk biscuit and ham-eating kind of country strength that usually turned his fights into straight beat downs, and most niggas didn't even get a chance to swing back. But Angel wasn't one of those niggas. He was a gladiator, and toe-to-toe was his specialty.

The cop recovered fast enough to duck the next blow, and at the same time, he swung his own right that caught the youngster's chin with an upper-cut. Angel might've been a little older and a tad bit slower, but he made up for that with experience. He was a brawler used to going ten rounds in rings with no refs and no rules.

The big boxers danced in slow circles around the lobby as they tried to feel each other out. Monsta's strength was easy to size-up, but his mental toughness was the question. Angel jabbed with his mouthpiece to expose any weaknesses.

"Fake-ass gorilla, you ain't nothing but a circus clown."

The sting of Angel's words was obvious. Monsta's blood boiled just like the cop thought it would. He knew exactly how to use the dummy's temper to keep him off balance.

Monsta threw a heavy left that missed too far to the right. Angel bipped and bopped with a quick shuffle of his feet, and then he released an ugly left-right-left flurry with some old-school sound effects, "Sss-Sss-Sss…" The combination dropped the flunky to one knee.

"You should've brought a pen and paper." The cop unwound another combo. "To take notes on this ass whoopin'."

Unfortunately for Angel, Monsta's skull was thicker than he thought it was, too hard hardheaded to go down that easily. The flunky's daze cleared just in time for him to tuck and roll before he got knocked out. A big fist flew past his face and skidded across the busted table behind him. Angel's "Sss-Sss" turned into a "Ssshit" as he pulled back his hand with no skin on his knuckles.

Monsta spotted a long rusty screw on the floor by the sofa. He cuffed it between his meaty fingers then jumped to his feet. The cop didn't see it, and when he moved in to deliver another knockout blow, a couple holes punched into his face forced him to rethink that tactic. Breathing hard from the sting, he looked around for the .40 he dropped, but Knuck had scooped that back in the first round.

Monsta wasn't giving the cop any more time to think about his next move. The goon smelled blood in the water, and he circled like a shark moving in for the kill. Angel threw a fake jab just to keep his distance, but he caught a vicious round house smack-dab in the kisser. It opened his bottom lip like a pussy, and it had him bleeding like it was that time of the month. Monsta's blow snatched the rug out from under the cop's feet, but before the youngster could press his advantage, Angel kicked him in the shin hard enough to break him down to the same level. Too close for punches, their ground-game took over.

They both threw elbows. Angel got an arm bar but couldn't hold it. Monsta went for a headlock but the cop twisted his way out. The brawlers tore at each other's faces with bloody fingers, poking at eyes with thumbs. Even their knees joined the fight, kicking at ribs, nuts, and any body part in reach. If their all-out brawl was a UFC fight, the judges would've scored them a draw. But they weren't in the UFC, and Knuck was the only judge that night.

Just as it seemed as if Angel was about to get the ups once again, Knuck brought his one-hit-wonder out of retirement. A nasty right-hook to the jaw instantly knocked the rest of the fight out of the cop, down goes Frazier.

"Y'all takin' too dam long. Fight over, nigga." Knuck snatched Monsta off the floor.

The flunky was breathing hard and bleeding heavy. His nose was a casualty of the close combat, and if Knuck hadn't been there to take the even out of the odds, Angel would've went undefeated, 2-0. But, of course, Monsta didn't see it that way.

"Told you I was gonna fuck dis nigga up." He stumbled to his feet and started stomping the cop's ears together with his size 15's.

"Uh-uh' Knuck ignored the dummy and went over to the one elevator that hadn't worked in years. He pried open the doors. "Bring that nigga over here."

"Cain't stand dis crooked muh-fucka." Monsta dragged the cop over by his ankles.

"Yeah, yeah, yeah. Let's do this shit so we can get the fuck outta here." Knuck bent down to get a good grip under Angel's shoulders. They swung the body back and forth for momentum.

"One-two-three."Angel tumbled down the elevator shaft like a two-hundred and fifty pound sack of dead-weight. Five-seconds and twelve floors later, his body kicked up a cloud of sixty-year-old dust at the bottom.

"Rest in pieces, muh-fucka." Monsta leaned out into the darkness to spit one time on the crooked cop's grave.

Knuck never liked to free-style when he did a hit. He always stuck to the plan. But after the cop dropped his banger, his plans got changed on the fly. Before Monsta could turn around, Knuck stopped him with a "Click-Clack" from Angel's .40. He barely gave the flunky time to feel the cold steel before he pumped a bullet in the back of his head. Knuck painted the elevator shaft with Monsta's brains, and a swift kick in his ass sent his body tumbling through the cloud of dust after the crooked cop.

Duke

# Chapter Twenty-Nine

Around the same time Angel and Monsta were making their landing at the bottom of the Fab 40's elevator shaft, an anonymous call came into crime stoppers.

"9-1-1, how may I direct your emergency?"

"I just saw a little girl being kidnapped," a woman's voice screamed frantically over the line. "Ain't no tellin' what's gonna happen to that girl."

The woman said her name was Laquisha, and she was a local resident with no criminal background, Sundae's idea, in case they needed her to testify later at Run Thang's trial.

"How do you know it was a kidnapping?" At first, the 9-1-1 operator sounded suspicious, as if she was expecting a crank-caller. Of course, that only made Laquisha turn up her attitude.

"Cuz he beat the shit outta her, that's how. Y'all gonna do something, or what?"

"Okay, okay," the operator finally took her information, though reluctantly, as though she had more important calls to take. "Can you give me a description? License plate?"

"Yeah, a blue Impala on rims, plate number 7-4-14." Laquisha read her lines from a piece of paper, provided by Fool of course.

The emergency call was routed to CPD instantly, but Sundae had her contacts hold off on putting an Amber alert out for Trix. At the time, Run was on some Rock-star shit at a casino, rolling through his third rack of chips on the craps table with Red blowing on the dice. Just in case the twin decided to tune-in to the evening news, which he never really did, she didn't want to take the chance he'd see his own face flashing across the screen, or recognize his whip mixed-up in a kidnapping.

The sexy detective had her little cousin hit up Run's inbox with a tease that would entice him to change his location from the casino back to the projects. And they needed to make that happen before she got her crew geared up and ready to go all-in on a mission.

Cheri: What's 2 it?

Other business had almost made Run Thang forget about the new talent he discovered earlier at the fish joint, but a flashback of her juicy little ass jogged his memory, and he let her know it.

Run: Fiend'n 4 that taste!

Cheri: Tweak on this...

Trix shot him a triple-feature to get his junky fix.

1. She posed beneath a sheet twisted around in a sexy position.

2. A tease of her laced up and looking gorgeous in a pink bra and panties.

3. A full-body shot, no imagination necessary.

Trix's last pic pulled Run Thang harder than crack pulled Pookie in New Jack City, and he was ready to chase her pussy straight to the gutter.

Run: I need to hit that!

Cheri: Can u beat it up?

Run: Like a heavyweight!

The conversation got filthy faster than a XXX chat room after 1:00am. But Run didn't do phone sex, and he didn't waste any time putting in his bid for some live action.

Run: Fuck session?

Cheri: Still got that cutie?

Run: U-ME-SHE?

Cheri: Fuck yeah! ☺! ☺! ☺!

Run Thang ditched his plans at the casino and Trix got scooped. Twenty miles and forty-five minutes later, they were all beating down the door to the groupie lounge with drinks in hands, pills popping, and a freaky script written just for them.

Inside Run's X-rated playpen, Trix wasted no time molesting the Suburban chick out of her Gucci buttons and Victoria Secret straps.

Then she cranked up her Cheri act with a strip tease for the twin who was behind the lens of a Sony HD with the "Record" light glowing red.

"Peel that shirt off, drop those shorts…" Run directed the action like a pervert in a porn video. "Smack that ass, grind those hips…" He kept the mega-pixels zoomed in tight on the two cuties tangled on the couch like a human pretzel.

Trix didn't mind showing off her talent, and she handled the freak in Red like the handlebars on a Kawasaki.

"Mmmm," the horny chick was loving her stunt work. "Oooh…" she squirmed under the pressure.

Trix hit the throttle on the girl's g-spot with a two-fingered grip and popped a wheelie with her thighs. But Red wanted to melt in Cheri's mouth, not in her hands, and she let her sexy rider know it.

"Lick it, suck it, bite it…"

Lucky for the cutie, Trix was a certified headhunter. She locked onto Red's candy-coated M&M like a Pit-bull locked onto a pork chop, and after a couple shakes of her head and a vicious grrrowl from her throat, she had the chick's body screaming.

"Damn." The sexy show had Run Thang charged up and starting to overheat.

No doubt, the twin was used to treating himself with more games and goodies than a pimp in a ho factory, but Cheri's action on Red was almost too much P for a playa. He kicked his jumpers into a corner, shook off his jeans, and lost his shirt somewhere behind him. Bullet wounds and tattoos weren't the only ways to tell the twins apart, Fool leaned slightly to the right, Run hung a little on the left.

Either way, Trix broke the code to keeping a trick like him treating without letting him taste her candy for real, and that time she intended to use Red's body as a blocker. Before her Cheri act started blowing the cutie's wig back, Run had already been playing tic-tac-toe on her brain cells with some X's and OC's, and at that moment she was spaced out and flying higher than an astronaut. Trix cocked back on Red's pretty thighs then split open her pink pussy with two fingers.

"Let me watch you beat it up." She led Run over to the couch by his ego.

The twin's dick looked stronger than Popeye's forearm, the twist in his dick could've been an elbow. He moved in with no hesitation and began putting a pounding on Red that almost had Trix impressed. In fact, if they had met under different circumstances, she would've loved to be a victim of his beat-down.

But Trix was big on safety, and strapping-up didn't seem to be a part of Run Thang's practice. Fucking a raw dick was a no-no, and besides, her role in Fool and Sundae's script was coming to an end.

While Run flexed his muscle inside of Red, Trix quietly slipped behind the Sony HD and ejected the memory card. The twin's blockbuster would never see the big-screen, not if she could help it.

# Chapter Thirty

Trix had her phone on speaker and laying on top of a table broadcasting the freak show live over the air waves. Fool and Knuck were tuned in while they sat incognito inside a rusty bucket parked in the lot. Meanwhile, Sundae was posted in the lobby right down the hall from the Groupie Lounge. "Beat it up" was their "go" word for the next stage of their operation.

Fool turned down the volume on his phone and then made sure the screen showed "mute" before giving cuz a nod. Knuck took his cue and dialed 9-1-1 on a cheap, pre-paid, $19.99 dollar store special. The line rung ten times and he damn near hung up, ready to redial, when the operator finally answered. Her voice was thick with smacking sounds, probably peanut butter and crackers.

"This is 9-1-1, please hold for the soonest available operator."

"Ain't no time to hold," Knuck cut in before the woman could click off the line.

"What's your emergency?" The operator didn't bother keeping her attitude polite. She was too pissed at having her snack interrupted.

"Just saw that little girl from the news," Knuck put just enough excitement in his voice to make him sound convincing.

"From the Amber alert?" The operator put just a little bit more professionalism in her voice, probably because she knew the call would be recorded and reviewed.

"Yeah, that one." The call was turning out to be longer than Knuck's patience. Besides recording his call, he knew it could probably be traced, too.

It didn't take long for Trix's kidnap to hit the police hot sheet. Besides Laquisha's report, an old couple who were on a tourist trip through the Windy City just happened to be stalled at the end of the bridge, and they witnessed a little girl being manhandled into the passenger side of a blue Chevy. The two frantic 9-1-1 calls got Sundae's cousin posted on every news station in Illinois.

Fool jabbed Knuck with an elbow to remind him, "No room for mistakes."

"Seen dude dragging her out of a blue Chevy." Knuck didn't need acting skills to read his lines. "He took her inside 1340 North Larrabee, apartment 1601.

"Are you sure that was her?" There was more smacking on the operator's end of the line. Knuck could almost smell Ritz crackers on her breath.

"Mann, my vision is 20/20. Heard some gunshots earlier, too. You might wanna tell tha police to check over in 1230."

"Can I get your name for Crime Stoppers?"

Fool cocked back another elbow, but that time, there was no need to pull the trigger.

"Hell naw. Just send the dam police." Knuck killed the call, snatched out the battery, and then slung the cheap phone out of the window.

Cuz had on gloves of course, leaving no prints, and even though that part of the job was done, the next stage was critical. So, they tuned back into the Groupie Lounge and turned the volume up.

"Nail that ass to those cushions. Don't let her sexy body run from you..." Trix was still working the action from behind the camera. "Throw some combos at that pussy. Left-right, uppercut it like Tyson."

In the background, Red was laying her vocals over a track of flesh on flesh, skin smacking skin, and hips pounding thighs.

"Sounds like Run has his slutty buddy cummin'." It wasn't Fool's first time overhearing his brother's work, and he still wasn't impressed.

"Yeah, sounds like he's servin' that bitch up like a flapjack." Knuck laughed at his own creativeness as he attempted to bring a soggy Swisher back to life with a lighter.

"I wasn't too quick to use baby gurl like cheese in a trap, tho." Just the thought of his twin pointing his dirty dick in shorty's direction had Fool's nerves wired tight and ready to snap.

Sundae wasn't taking any chances either. While the rest of her crew was on standby a few blocks away, she picked a spot in the Fab 40 where she could stay close to her little cousin. She was even listening in on the action through a conference call ready to spring the trap.

"From what you tellin' me, it was her hat-trick to pull in the first place, and can't nobody slip a banana in the nigga's tailpipe better than a pro." Knuck was thinking the same thoughts as his cousin, but without the feelings. He'd only met Trix in person once, but Fool filled him in on shorty's qualifications.

"Yeah, well, he better bust that last nut, 'cause the only fuckin he doin' after this is wit punk's in the joint. And he might get caught on the wrong end of that position…" Fool's words were cut off when the tone of Trix's voice suddenly changed on her end of the line. The twin and Knuck instantly killed their jokes and laughs.

"Baby gurl, it's yo turn to ride this dick." Run's invite for Trix to join in on the action was met with tension on all three ends of the conference call.

Knowing his brother the way he did, Fool knew that wasn't a request, but more like a "Bitch, get your ass over here." Run also wasn't known for taking "no" for an answer.

"Why don't you strap on one of these rubbers first?" Everyone caught the stress in Trix's voice, as though she was stalling for time but running out of hurdles to throw in front of the nigga to slow him down.

"I don't do rubbers, shawty. You about to get this dick raw-dawg, Doberman Pincher.

Somewhere up on the top floor, Sundae's worry shifted into panic-mode, and that forced her to make a mistake.

"I'm moving in," her voice came in loud and clear over the conference call, and that was the problem. Her phone was supposed to be on mute, since Trix's was on speaker. Sundae had just let Run in on the conversation, and he didn't miss a word either.

"Bitch, what tha fuck is that?" The twin could be heard scrambling for the phone. After a few more "Bitches" and "Ho's," then what sounded like a loud "Smack," the line went dead.

"Sundae, I'm on the way," Fool shouted into his phone but forgot his was on mute. His fingers fumbled to swipe at the screen as Knuck beat him out of the car.

The cousins jetted across the lot on full after burner. Fool gripped a baby 9, while Knuck hauled on a 357 magnum. Inside the Fab 40, they skidded to a stop at the elevators just as one of the locals was hopping a ride going up. She was an old lady struggling with a shopping cart and a seeing-eye-dog on a leash.

"Auntie, why don't you catch the next ride?" Fool politely excused her from the elevator while Knuck stabbed at the button for the top floor. There was no room for passengers on their trip, and no time for stops either.

On the way up, Fool speed-dialed Sundae, but his frustration started to boil over when he couldn't get any bars.

"Damn, G. Can't get no signal." He didn't give up though, and his fingers kept tapping at the screen.

Luckily, no one was waiting for an elevator on any of the other floors and they quickly passed the seventh, eighth, and then the ninth when Sundae's phone finally rang.

"Fool, hold on," her answer sounded winded, as if she had just made a mad dash to the apartment. In the background, the butt of her .40 pounded on the door. "Police. Open up."

# Chapter Thirty-One

"Fool, where you at?" Sundae was still pounding on the door, frantic to get inside and get Trix out.

"We almost there, hold…" Fool's voice faded as Sundae took the phone away from her ear.

Trix screamed. "Help. Rape. This nigga crazy."

"What? Rape? Bitch, you crazy." Run Thang's response was followed by the sound of a heavy punch, and then the thump of a body hitting the floor.

Thoughts of what was happening to her little cousin had Sundae's nerves wound tight and her trigger finger twitching. She hammered the door with the heavy .40, Bam. Bam. Bam.

A few tense seconds passed before Run shouted, "Who the fuck is it?" Locks clicked and the door was snatched open.

Run Thang stood in his jumpers and a pair of shorts, no shirt or socks, and his face was balled into a mask of rage as he sized up Sundae in the hallway.

"Bitch, you lost or something?" He didn't even bother looking at the Glock pointed at his chest.

"Get on the floor, now." Sundae's gun was steady, and her trigger finger tight.

Trix kneeled on the floor a few steps behind the twin, sobbing, shirt and skirt torn from her body. She glanced up towards the door with a hand covering one eye. That side of her face was already starting to swell and turn colors.

"Motherfucker." Sundae lost it. She rushed into the apartment, police training be damned. But, at the same time, she knew Fool and Knuck would be there to back her up any second.

Run Thang was light on his feet though, and his mentality was always on offense, never defense. He caught Sundae by surprise as he leaned forward to meet her rush, and he grabbed her hand holding the gun. His fingers clamped down tighter than a Kung-Fu grip, and with a quick twist sideways, he forced the detective to her knees.

"Ooooww!" Pain shot through Sundae's wrist with the sizzle of a lightning bolt. Run Thang snatched the gun out of her numbed fingers.

No way did he believe the bitch on her knees in front of him was really a cop. He was thinking robbery, not raid. He reached down, grabbed Sundae by her strawberry-blond locks, and lifted her head back.

"Bitch, what kinda setup is this?" It was more of an accusation than a question, and it wouldn't be the first time Run foiled someone's stunt to catch him slipping.

"Bastard." Sundae started to spit up into the twin's face, but his grip on her hair choked it off.

"Huh, bitch? Can't you hear?" He smacked her across the face with the .40's sharp butt, instantly splitting open a bloody gash along the detective's cheek.

"You and that lil slut thought y'all had an easy vic?" Run cut his words short when the elevator rumbled and squealed to a stop down the hall.

The distraction forced Run to hesitate, giving Sundae the split second she needed. Her hand slid towards one of her ankles and a .32 snub she kept for backup situations just like that one.

Unfortunately, Run Thang's P's and Q's were too sharp to miss a move like that. His instincts were honed in the projects, where every move made was a matter of life and death, and it damn sure wasn't his day to die.

The twin ducked behind the wall in the kitchen as Sundae's .32 came up bucking. her move was quick, but his trigger finger was quicker. Run bent his arm around the wall and jagged the first three rounds from the Glock's clip. Bullets flew every which way through the tiny apartment, his and hers, penetrating walls, windows, and couch cushions.

Cutie Red screamed at the top of her lungs but sat frozen in her spot. Trix knew better, and she found a hiding spot behind the Lay-Z-Boy. The "whoop whoop" of sirens outside had Run Thang rethinking his strategy. Maybe that bitch really was a cop, and holding court inside the Groupie Lounge was a death trap.

Sundae's 32 only had six rounds, and her trigger finger paused after her first few shots. That was what Run was waiting for. The twin came up busting as he dove out of the kitchen, through the door, and then out into the hallway where he disappeared.

Down the breezeway, at that same time, the elevator doors were finally sliding open. Fool and Knuck rushed out, pistols pointed and ready to pop. When they rounded the corner to the Groupie Lounge's door, they quickly spotted Sundae lying on the floor, curled into a ball of pain, and holding her stomach. Red was over on the couch still screaming, and still naked. Trix was just then creeping out of her hiding spot, crawling her way towards Sundae.

"Sundae," Trix screamed. She was the first to spot the bright-red blood leaking between her cousin's clamped fingers.

"That bastard shot me," Sundae's words came out in a breathless groan of agony.

Fool and Knuck leaned down and forced her hands away from her stomach so they could get a better look at the wound. it looked bad, and she was bleeding heavily. Luckily, the police outside would be up any moment, and an ambulance was always just a few minutes away from the projects.

"Which way did he go?" No way did Fool want to leave Sundae's side, but him and Knuck probably didn't want to be there when her back-up arrived, especially not with her shot and them holding two bangers. He definitely wasn't about to let his brother get away, either.

"I don't know." Sundae breathed through clenched teeth, and the pain twisting her stomach muscles wouldn't let her say any more.

The look on Trix's face said she didn't know which way Run Thang ran. Red was still screaming.

"Hold on, baby gurl. Hold on," Fool wiped at the bloody gash on Sundae's cheek. He stood up, and then grabbed Knuck by the sleeve. "Time to pop smoke."

The cousins made their exit. No doubt, the police would put the projects on lockdown, and they didn't want to be a pair of guinea pigs for their interrogation tactics. Plus, Fool had an idea where Run might've disappeared to. He led the way to the stairwell.

# Chapter Thirty-Two

Fool and Knuck navigated the back steps with their safeties off and fingers itching triggers. A few landings down, they had to elbow their way past a private party of dope fiends tying each other off and hunting for veins with needles. All of their irritated faces told a silent tale of being interrupted one too many times. Run Thang must've just jetted past them. The cousins shifted gears to catch up.

Almost at the first floor, a traffic jam of cluckers were tussling over the last sizzle on a crack pipe. Fool was in the lead and was the first to bust through the mob. One of the old-heads didn't recognize the twin and he was bold enough to complain.

"Hey, man, watch where..."

"Fuck outta tha way." A shove from Knuck bounced the man off a wall. A toothless hooker camouflaged in filth was smart enough to take advantage of the commotion. She snatched the one-hitter and took off up the steps.

"Bitc.!" The crowd scrambled to keep up, hot on her heels.

Fool hopped over a bum passed out on the last landing, and he damn near slipped in a puddle of piss, but Knuck was there just in time for the catch. Finally on the first floor, and out of breath, leg muscles burning from their calves all the way up to their ass cheeks, they spotted the basement door cracked open. Run Thang couldn't have been more than a minute ahead of them.

"Cut that," Fool struggled to talk. "Nigga off." He was bent over with both hands on his hips. "At 1230."

There wasn't much gas left in Knuck's tank either, but he nodded "Aight" then broke for the backdoor.

"Hold on," Fool held out his hand to stop him, trying to warn him, but it was too late. Knuck was already out of sight. The police had already flooded through the Fab 40's front, and once they hit the back, shit would get tight on cuz.

Fool stepped into the stairwell going down. All the way at the bottom, a single light bulb buzzed on its last leg and barely pushed back the darkness in the basement. The twin's senses were forced to adapt quickly. His eyes adjusted to the dim light, a few feet in his nose wrinkled at the smell of rotting garbage, and his ears picked up the sound of rats fighting over scraps.

Fool's Jordan's dropped from the last step and splashed in a puddle of sewage slick with mildew. That was his first mistake; he was moving too fast and not thinking fast enough. If Run had been laying a trap, he would've just bit a bullet.

While he struggled to steady his breathing and let his endurance catch up, he hit a mental reset button on his thoughts. Run had to dash the same obstacle course that he just did, and knowing the way his brother liked to pop pills, Fool would bet a rack to a gallon of water that his radiator was about to overheat. Even so, there was no telling how much wind was left in that .40's clip, and trying to run his twin down on wobbly legs, temper steaming with thoughts of revenge, was a recipe for disaster.

A lighter flicked and a flame flared a few feet to Fool's right, He spun around with his aim low. a bum crouched in a corner cooking a meal of heroin in a tablespoon.

"H-h-hold on," the frightened fiend's bloodshot eyes bugged at the 9mm pointed straight at his face. His shaky hands struggled not to spill his only hit.

"Almost knocked yo wig off." Fool hissed at the old-timer.

"H-h-he went dat'away." the man's head nodded behind him toward the back wall.

Fool didn't hesitate. To catch up with his twin, he had to navigate around the hobo's camp, a bunch of milk crates and paint buckets filled with canned goods, and a dusty wardrobe he shared with a family of rats and their litter. He danced around a jumble of live wires crisscrossing the floor like a giant spider web, and then jumped over a big pile of shit. Whoever tried stripping those wires for the copper must have gotten the shit shocked out of them.

Way back when Al Capone still chased Bugsy through the streets with Tommy guns, hidden tunnels zig-zagged beneath the Old Town neighborhood Cabrini Green was built over. And way back before the twins ever stepped foot in the projects, someone had bashed-in the basements back wall to gain access to the underground hideout for conducting gang meetings, committing an occasional rape, or to dump a body with no witnesses.

The tunnels were known only as the tombs by the residents, and the only light that leaked in came from the basements buzzing bulb. Barely a few feet inside, Fool had to tap the flashlight app on his phone – sudden movement caught his attention.

"What tha…"A woman's frantic whisper hissed somewhere to the left. "Here come somebody else."

Fool lit her up with his phone. It was the hype, Vicky, and she was bent over, raggedy jeans down around her ankles while Ghost the fiend nailed her from the back.

"Hey, youngsta." Ghost's face cracked open in a toothless grin. "What up tho?" His crusty hips kept pounding at Vicky's ash-black ass without breaking his rhythm.

"Where Run go?" Any other time, Fool would've snapped a pic and made them famous on YouTube. Instead, he dropped the light and shook the mental image from his memory.

"Mmm," Vicky was feeling the old man. "That way." She nodded her head.

"How long?" Fool tried not to imagine how many diseases they must have been swapping.

"Uhh, uhh," Ghost humped and grunted like a dog in heat. "H-h-he j-just…" He was about to bust a nut.

"That's aight." Fool spun off before they started spraying body fluids.

Once upon a time, the tombs branched in every direction, for thousands of feet, until the city eventually blocked them off with tons of concrete and turned them into hundreds of dead ends. Fool knew them all. They were his tunnels, after all. But even so, he moved cautiously, step by step, his Mike's stepped over old liquor bottles and rusty beer cans. A foot kicked an old bullet no one even made guns for anymore.

At that point, Fool couldn't risk using his flashlight app that deep in the tunnels, or else he would've made himself a bulls-eye in the darkness. In about fifty feet, he knew there would be a left bend that quickly turned into a sharp-right, and then into a long stretch. That would be the next time he could expect to see light before reaching 1230, and that was if Run didn't get there first and knock out the bulb.

But, if Knuck got there in time, Fool knew cuz would turn Run Thang's lights out first. His brother might be aware of the tail chasing him from behind, but he didn't have a clue about the trap he was running into.

Feet splashed through a puddle somewhere up ahead. Run? Knuck? Or another bum? Fool almost out-reacted his own instincts with a shout, but he cut it off. Instead, he kicked his jumpers into high-gear. He banked into the slight bend, made the sharp right, then, bam, bam, bam, bullets shattered the ancient bricks, spraying fragments so close they scraped gouges across the side of his face.

Fool's eyes were finally adjusting to the darkness, but the .40 flashes fucked that up. And the tunnels made the rounds sound like shotgun blasts. His ears were ringing.

There was no time to recover, though. And, besides, the best defense was always a good offense. The twin cupped his hands and shouted to keep Run from getting a lock on his position.

"You missed me."

"Oh yeah?" Run's words were strained and out of breath, as if he was running a marathon.

Run Thang's shots were just a test-fire, hopefully to slow Fool down. He needed a breather to give himself time to press his own reset button. Almost catching his twin face-first in the trap would've been a bonus. The bullets came a couple inches from shattering Fool's skull.

"Stick yo head around the corner one more time." Run was too winded to realize his voice broadcasted his coordinates like a GPS signal. His brother did, though. Bam. Bam. Fool let off a couple rounds of his own artillery. He knew his shots were misses, but his words wouldn't be.

"No flunkie to back yo punk ass up."

"He prob'ly," Bam. Bam. "Havin' fun wit yo bitch." Bam. Bam. "Again."

Run's bullets ricocheted all over the place, and they forced Fool to crouch low to duck a lucky hit. The .40 flashes measured the distance between them at about thirty feet.

"Naw, I put ya boy on a milk carton, missing person." Fool didn't give him the update on Angel. He kept that as a surprise for later, when Run found out he was being charged with the cop's murder.

Run Thang took advantage of their conversation and made a dash for the exit. Fool fired at the sound of his running feet. Bam. Bam. Jammed.

Damn. Fool tried jacking the slide to see what was the hang-up, but no good. He still couldn't use his flashlight app, so he couldn't see shit. At least his shots stopped Run from running.

Next, Fool hesitated for a second, long enough to give his eyes a chance to readjust, and for the bells to stop ringing in his ears. His brother had no way of knowing he was jammed-up, or that he knew Sundae's .40 was a mini with only ten shots, so he used that inside info to lay his own trap.

"You runnin' from this fight?" Fool stayed low to the ground as he peeped around the corner.

"Fuck you." Bam. Bam. Click.

"Uh-oh," Fool paused for a couple heartbeats to let Run's predicament sink in. "You outta ammo?"

"Clips fo days," Run lied.

"Put 'em down and knuckle up."

Silence. The only sound was water dripping somewhere from a leaky pipe. Fool fished for something else to get under his twin's skin with.

"Can't fight under the influence?"

More silence. Drip-drip-drip.

"Getting pimped by the police got yo knuckles soft?"

"Fuck you, nigga." Run slung the empty .40 at Fool's head.

Got'em. Fool moved in low, trying to get a lock on his brother's outline in the darkness. The light coming from ahead was worse than what he left behind. The bulb in 1230 flickered on and off like a strobe light, and the effect made every move slow-motion, ghetto special effects.

At first, the twins squared off like two gorillas sizing each other up. Fool didn't need light to see that Run was still under the influence. He could smell it in his sweat. He measured his reach with a couple of jabs.

Run Thang didn't need to see Fool's face to read his emotions. he could feel the heat of his brother's temperature. And he knew how to get under his skin, too.

"You lucky yo bitch didn't bleed-out."

"You about to hang for that." Fool stepped in with a right-left-right combo, but Run bipped and bopped out of his reach.

"Catchin' comes befo the hangin'." Run Thang wasn't too high to tell Fool was just feeling him out with his maneuver. So he played along, pretending to be slow to react and making it seem as though he were higher than he really was.

It had been years since the twins scrapped against each other, way back when they were still pee-wees exercising their gangsta on

198

local chumps. But they never forgot the outcomes of those matches. Fool always had the finest footwork between the two, and he was quick to knuckle-up toe to toe. On the other side of the ring, Run's scouting report was all backyard WWE, ground and pound.

RunThang acted as if he barely recovered from Fool's neat miss, and he threw a wild punch on purpose. If he could draw his twin in, he could wrap him up.

"Thought you was hittin' that weight yard?" Run leaned back on his foot to set up his move.

"I was," Fool stepped in to sweep his brother's front foot with a slick leg.

Run got off a left hook followed by a right, but his knuckles barely scraped skin, because Fool was waiting on that bullshit. He didn't expose that hand though, and instead he stumbled backwards off balance as though the combo really faded him.

Bait like that was irresistible to a wrestler, and as usual, Run Thang was out-thinking himself by thinking he was really out thinking Fool. He dipped in low to wrap-up his twin's legs, but his reaction times were a half-second behind on the shot clock, and he fucked around and caught a knee to his face. Solid.

Run fell back on his ass, but not before grabbing a fistful of Fool's shirt, and they both hit the floor together. Then their bodies tumbled and twisted in a swinging storm of knuckles, elbows, and stiff-arms. Momentum carried them both through the crumbling wall underneath 1230.

Run sunk his teeth into Fool's shoulder.

"Ahhh!"

He shook him like a pit bull on a pork chop.

"Grrr!"

Fool's instincts unwound a chop that cracked his twin in the throat. Run spit him out coughing and choking, but at the same time he responded with a knee to his brother's nuts.

"Uggh!" All the air rushed out of Fool's lungs, and he tossed up his last meal in a spray of chunks. Then he curled into a ball like a baby, fighting for breath.

"Muhfucka," Run took advantage and climbed on top. He unwound, about to take off on Fool with a flurry of fists, but sudden footsteps sneaking up behind him canceled his flight plan.

Cold steel tapped Run on the back of his head, and then a hammer "click-clacked" on something heavy.

"Gotta wanted poster wit yo name on it." Knuck's trigger finger flexed. "Dead or alive."

"Hold up," Fool reached out a frantic hand to stop him.

"We got..." His words came out in gasps. "El Jefe..." He coughed and spit. "To handle that dirty work."

Knuck sucked his teeth as he contemplated. He wanted to off that nigga so bad he could taste it, and he was blood-thirsty.

"That's right," cuz lowered the banger while Fool climbed to his feet spitting out the foul taste of vomit. "You got reservations down-state, eight-by-ten with some Puerto Ricans."

Run was boxed-in and cornered, but he still had room to shake off the threat.

"Run Thang runs joints, too." He wheezed out a laugh that creased his face with a more serious look. "This shit ain't over."

"Oh yeah?" Fool had a parting gift for his twin, a print of Michael Jordon floating from the free-throw line, against his face. "Take that wit'cha."

# Chapter Thirty-Three

Fool and Knuck stepped out onto the tenth-floor breezeway of the Carter just as a motorcade of news teams began rolling in. Channels 2, 5, 7, and 9, and even Univision was representing. Their cameras had the area lit up like a night game at the Bears stadium, and the police lights strobed off the buildings with the effect of a giant disco ball. But the only music at the moment was the chop-chop of helicopters hovering high in the air.

Turned out, Tuffy was in his cell down-state and watching the "breaking news" live. The old P.R. reached out through a three-way almost right away, and Fool gave him the inside scoop on current events without giving away the whole plot over the phone.

"Man, Papa, you're slicker than I thought you were." Tuffy was definitely impressed.

"I had a lil help." Fool had Knuck stick around with Run knocked-out and hog-tied, while he rendezvoused with one of Sundae's teammates to make sure they didn't overlook his twin during their sweep of the buildings.

"I'm not sure if those charges are gonna stick, though." Fool did his part, as promised, but he wasn't making any guarantees.

Surveillance cameras had caught their staged kidnapping from four different angles with a view of Run Thang's face that was sharper than a Blue ray at 1080p, and they even took snapshots of his license plates. To make Run's predicament a little stickier, after doming Monsta and Angel, Knuck slipped the crooked cop's gun inside his apartment and hid it where it would be easy to find.

Run Thang was going to need more luck than a leprechaun to twist his way out of Fool and Sundae's plot. Even so, there was no way of knowing for sure how his story would end. He might pull an O.J. Simpson, if the glove don't fit, must acquit.

"Plus, that nigga has his own help." Fool had already told Tuffy about the crooked cops.

"Don't worry about it, papa." El Jefe could only say so much on his end of the line, but his meaning was still easy to get "He won't make it to see a trial."

Run Thang never got much love outside of Cabrini, and the Gangstas in the county jail wouldn't be too quick to back him up when the Puerto Ricans started pulling out their swords.

"Just keep me posted." As far as Fool was concerned, Run could rot in a cell or a grave, and he didn't give a fuck which one.

"No doubt. I'll tell Loc' to move you out of the red and back into the black." Tuffy let Fool know his sacrifice was appreciated, and then he killed the call before the Illinois Department of Corrections could record too much of their conversation.

Knuck nudged Fool with an elbow, and with a nod of his head drew the twin's attention over to the back of the Himalaya where a team of coroners were wheeling out a body bag, probably Angel or Monsta. Thankfully, Sundae wouldn't be one of those DOA statistics. The same S.I.U. cop who helped Fool tag Run Thang also gave him an update on the detective's condition. Her stomach wound looked worse than it was. Even so, Fool kept his fingers crossed for her prognosis.

Trix and Red were escorted to the district's headquarters-cuffed in the back of a squad car, and before the night was over, they would most definitely get the riot act from police interrogators. Sundae's little cousin wasn't new to their tactics, and Fool wasn't worried about her busting under that pressure.

The cute suburban chick was a different story. Knuck voted to axe Run's only witness, but Fool vetoed that bill. Red's self-worth was already worthless, and her system was pumped full of so many drugs her testimony would be worth even less.

"Think those nigga's in the 40 gonna take this shit layin down?" Knuck knew better than to underestimate the loyalty of Run's crew. Monsta wasn't that nigga's only go-getter.

"Probably not, but they'll pick another head to run that body." Some of those same go-getters used to be part of Fool's crew, and they never forgot that he was the man with the plan. Once their pockets were flat long enough, they would eventually fall back in line.

"In the meantime," True to Fool's M.O., his thoughts were already switching to other business. "We got one more loose-end to tie up."

The other day, Tameeka woke in the hospital, and the doctors were about ready to sign off on her walking papers. Even though her body was healing just fine, her mind still couldn't shake the flashbacks of her rape. During his last visit, Fool left her with a promise to kill that nightmare once and for all.

Duke

## Chapter Thirty-Four

The only way Creep's recent run of luck could've been described was "from rags to riches." After Monsta gave him a hundred and twenty singles, along with a pocket full of change for his troubles, he went on a spending spree, and didn't waste any time spoiling himself with goodies.

The only thing the retard loved more than Twinkies and jerking his little dick to porn was the satisfying rush of nicotine hitting his system. So, instead of copping a bunch of loosies from the poor hustlers under the building, he decided to splurge on a whole pack of Newport's.

Creep's very next purchase turned out to be a big mistake. For him and Dead eye's dinner that night, he bought a jumbo pack of hot dogs from a Korean minimart. He learned the hard way not to do that shit again. The cheap greasy meat gave his little buddy the runs for two days straight.

Then, a couple of days ago, the boy ran into the shoe man selling twenty dolla hollas out of his trunk, and he copped himself a pair of Knock-off white pleather Chucks, "Made in Nigeria". Creep broke them in running from security at a downtown dollar store during an attempt to stuff a set of paint markers down the front of his pants. An hour later, with red swooshes on the side and a crooked Jump man on each tongue, the retard showed off his fly Chucks all over the projects.

"Ca-ca-can I getta l-l-light?" Creep stopped in front of a small crowd of knuckleheads who were hanging in the Himalaya's lobby, flipping 40's and shooting dice for dollars. Dead Eye learned the hard way to keep its distance around strangers, and it ducked out of sight behind the boy's legs.

"Let me get one of'em." A youngster with his hat broke to the back and crying tatted tears leaned against a wall flicking a lighter.

"Fi-Fi-Fitty cent." Creep was retarded, not stupid.

"I gotta quarter," The knucklehead patted his pockets, pretending to search for some more change, and then his hand shot out - "Gimme this shit." He snatched the cigarette out of the boy's surprised fingers.

"Now catch up wit yo crowd, goofy." The young bully's partners paused their dice game long enough to laugh and claim shorts on the Newport.

"I hate you." Creep snatched on Dead eye's leash, and then took flight through the lobby before they decided to beat him up and see what else he had worth taking.

The odd pair of buddies broke right past the elevators, around the wall of mail boxes, and to the back steps where Creep finally slammed on the brakes when he realized nobody had bothered to chase them.

"Pssst." The sound almost made the boy and his mutt jump out their skins, and fur.

Knuck emerged from the darkness in the stairwell like a ghost dressed in all black. Creep's nerves relaxed a little bit, but not Dead eye's. The dog knew better.

"Got something fo'ya" Knuck held a Black & Mild between his fingers, and he motioned for the retard to come over.

"Ain't none of that jungle weed is it?" Creep looked suspicious.

The boy wasn't new to the sweet-smelling cigars, and recently, he even had a chance to pull on one that was stuffed with that "Weed" he had been hearing so many people talk about. The Black had him high for two days in a row, and since he didn't believe a weed grown in the projects could make him so dizzy, he figured it must've been a jungle weed.

"Even better." Knuck didn't know what the fuck the retard was talking about. He held out the Black with one hand and sparked a lighter with his other.

For Creep, something for nothing usually turned out to be a dumb idea, and when he looked down at Dead Eye, even the mutt's face seemed to be saying the same thing. But the boy had never been good at standing up to peer pressure, not because he was curious, but because it was easier than getting his lights punched out. So, he accepted the cigar with nervous fingers and raised it to his lips while Knuck torched the tip with a flame.

A couple puffs was all it took for Creep to dig the flavor, not minty like a Newport, but sweet like an apple. The tobacco was kind of moist though, and hard to hit, so he pulled harder and held in the smoke hoping to get the nicotine rush he loved so much. A few seconds in, the boy looked up and was just about to tell Knuck how good the Black tasted, but for some strange reason, the words got stuck on the tip of his tongue and wouldn't come off.

Creep struggled to shake the crazy feeling, to cough, open his mouth and spit, but his body refused to respond. The retard never had many brain cells to work with in the first place, and the PCP-laced cigar lit a fuse to what he had left. They exploded all at once like millions of tiny firecrackers on a 4th of July celebration. Suddenly, nothing seemed to make any sense. Shapes changed and colors shifted, as if he had stepped out of reality and inside of a spooky cartoon.

The boy stood frozen in his tracks as Knuck seemed to melt in front of his terrified eyes and transform into something like the Incredible Hulk. The big goon's muscle grew and grew, ripping through his clothes, and even his skin turned green, the color of snot. Then the nightmare's mouth stretched open, revealing a set of needle-sharp fangs.

Creep had seen enough of that bullshit, and his instincts kicked into panic-mode. He dropped Dead Eye's leash like a dead weight and took off running, first down the hallway, then past the elevators and into the front stairwell. His legs pumped so fast the floors seemed to pass by in one long blur, 5th, 7th, 9th… He glanced back to see Dead Eye hot on his heels, except in his hallucination, the dog wasn't his faithful best friend, but a one-eyed jackal from the pits of hell. The mutt's ears were long, pointy horns, and its canines were fangs dripping with poison. Dead Eye was a beast.

Creep shifted gears and peeled rubber on his Chucks. The $12^{th}$, $14^{th}$, and $16^{th}$ landings rushed by, and he didn't stop until the building ran out of floors and he landed on the roof. Then he tried slamming the access door behind him, but the jackal was too fast. Dead Eye was right there.

"Please don't eat me," Creep backed away slowly, hands raised and begging. "Please don't eat me."

Suddenly, a flock of green flying goblins swooped down from purple clouds hanging low in the sky. The rooftop was crawling with slithering snakes, furry rats, and slimy cockroaches. The boy ducked and dodged the monsters lurking at the edge of his vision, all waiting to reach out and snatch him up. Then he tripped and fell hard on his ass, and the evil jackal walked towards him, wagging its tail. Dead Eye licked him across his face.

"Please don't eat me, please don't eat me…" The green Hulk stepped out of the stairwell and onto the rooftop. Creep's fingernails dug frantically into the black tar as he crawled over toward the edge looking for a way to escape. Sixteen stories down, the people looked like ants scurrying across the ground.

"Told you that shit was good. Makes you wanna fly, don't it?" Knuck picked up Dead Eye's leash and wrapped it in his hand.

"Fly? Like a bird?" Creep was stuck way past stupid. His head swiveled on his shoulders, first looking up at Knuck, then down over the roof, and back up at Knuck.

The thought of flying reminded the retard of an Animal Planet episode he had recently watched. A momma bird forced the baby bird to learn how to fly by kicking it out of the nest, fly or die. Knuck must've seen that same episode, because before Creep could turn back around, the big goon planted a size 12 Nike print in the crack of his ass and kicked him over the edge.

For some strange reason though, the boy didn't feel as if he was falling. In fact, to his surprise, he really could fly. With his arms out wide and flapping, just like that baby chick fresh out of the nest, Creep flew straight towards the ground. Too bad Dead Eye didn't have wings like he did, the retard thought. The dusty mutt fell right past him going every bit of a hundred miles an hour, its mouth open in a silent bark. Creep watched as his buddy's frizzy fur splattered all over the concrete, right before he did.

*To Be Continued...*
Gangsta City 2
Coming Soon

## Coming Soon From Lock Down Publications

LOVE KNOWS NO BOUNDRIES III

By **Coffee**

GANGSTA CITY II

By **Teddy Duke**

A DANGEROUS LOVE VII

By **J Peach**

BURY ME A G III

By **Tranay Adams**

BLOOD OF A BOSS III

By **Askari**

THE KING CARTEL III

By **Frank Gresham**

CLOSED LEGS DON'T GET FED &

SHE DON'T DESERVE THE D

By **Reds Johnson**

THESE NIGGAS AIN'T LOYAL III

By **Nikki Tee**

BROOKLYN ON LOCK II

By **Sonovia Alexander**

THE STREETS BLEED MURDER II

By **Jerry Jackson**

DIRTY LICKS II

By **Peter Mack**

THE ULTIMATE BETRAYAL II

By **Phoenix**

Gangsta City

CONFESSIONS OF A DOPEMAN'S DAUGHTER

By **Rasstrina**

<u>**Available Now**</u>

LOVE KNOWS NO BOUNDARIES **I & II**

By **Coffee**

SILVER PLATTER HOE **I & II**

By **Reds Johnson**

A DANGEROUS LOVE **I, II, III, IV, V, VI**

By **J Peach**

CUM FOR ME

An **LDP Erotica Collaboration**

THE KING CARTEL **I & II**

By **Frank Gresham**

BLOOD OF A BOSS **I & II**

By **Askari**

BURY ME A G **I & II**

By **Tranay Adams**

THESE NIGGAS AIN'T LOYAL **I & II**

By **Nikki Tee**

THE STREETS BLEED MURDER

By **Jerry Jackson**

DIRTY LICKS

By **Peter Mack**

THE ULTIMATE BETRAYAL

By **Phoenix**

BROOKLYN ON LOCK

By **Sonovia Alexander**

SLEEPING IN HEAVEN, WAKING IN HELL **I, II & III**

By **Forever Redd**

THE DEVIL WEARS TIMBS **I, II & III**

By **Tranay Adams**

DON'T FU#K WITH MY HEART **I & II**

By **Linnea**

BOSS'N UP **I & II**

By **Royal Nicole**

LOYALTY IS BLIND

By **Kenneth Chisholm**

A HUSTLA'Z AMBITION **I & II**

By **Damion King**

## <u>BOOKS BY LDP'S CEO, CA$H</u>

TRUST NO MAN

TRUST NO MAN 2

TRUST NO MAN 3

BONDED BY BLOOD

SHORTY GOT A THUG

A DIRTY SOUTH LOVE

THUGS CRY

THUGS CRY 2

TRUST NO BITCH

TRUST NO BITCH 2

TRUST NO BITCH 3

TIL MY CASKET DROPS

**Coming Soon**

TRUST NO BITCH (KIAM EYEZ' STORY)

THUGS CRY 3

BONDED BY BLOOD 2

Duke

Made in the USA
Monee, IL
05 March 2021

62045518R00118